Contents

Prologue

I hate being shot at.

Even more so, when the would-be assassin is any good and actually manages to hit his target.

Perversely though, I do take some comfort in the consistent predictability of the process.

I've had my share of upset plans and unexpected life-changing events.

It's good to know there are some things that still follow the blueprint.

The squeeze of the trigger. The hammer striking. The sound of the powder exploding to propel the bullet down the barrel. The whistle as the hot slug slices through the air, on its way to its target.

Me.

Finally, the moment of impact as the speeding sliver of metal punches its way through clothing, skin, bone and anything else which tries to bring it to a halt.

Bang. Ouch. Simple.

So here I lie, my faith in the stability of the Universe once again justified.

All it cost me is a hole in my arm and the blood which is trickling between my fingers and down the sleeve of another ruined shirt.

It's just as well I heal quickly.

But I'm getting ahead of myself

1

Chapter 1

My name is Jack, and I'm a fatalist. That's something like a pessimist, but not so downbeat.

I've been on this planet long enough to realise that life can, and will, throw your plans out of the window and turn your world upside-down, at a moment's notice. There's nothing you can do to stop it. All you can do is pick yourself up and have another go.

I encountered my first major setback as a teenager.

In the early 20's, the World cowered in the shadow of a possible extinction event. A large celestial mass was approaching the Earth.

Despite conspiracy theorists predicting it for the past twenty years, it apparently took astronomers by surprise.

The most technologically advanced nations threw themselves into a frenzy of collaboration. Even so, there seemed to be no overall agreement on what action to take. After so many science-fiction films dealing with the subject, it seemed unbelievable that there was no concrete plan in place to avoid the annihilation of all life on the planet.

Finally, in the absence of a unanimous decision, the United

States forged ahead with its own plan. Just like the movies. And, of course, the plan involved a large nuclear device.

Granted, as far as saving the planet, the mission was a success.

Unfortunately, a breakaway fragment of the rock still managed to enter the Earth's atmosphere.

At 25 metres across, it was slightly larger than the Chelyabinsk meteor of 2013. When it exploded in the air at an altitude of less than 20 kilometers, the energy from the blast exceeded 500 kilotons.

Like its predecessor, it caused incalculable devastation on the ground.

Less than two seconds after the explosion, most of the West Yorkshire city of Leeds was reduced to rubble.

I was living in Leeds at the time, with my parents.

Good news, I was on a college trip to London on that day.

Bad news, my parents were at home.

The loss of life was unimaginable. The US President expressed her condolences but never actually apologised. She used terms like 'collateral damage' and 'rational transactions'.

My parents, along with thousands of other victims were reduced to nothing more than percentages. Compared to the number of lives saved, they were insignificant.

But they, and the life I had known, were still gone.

The World reacted swiftly, aid pouring in from all nations. In the immediate aftermath, everyone wanted to be seen to be helping.

Later, of course, public interest waned, and reality began to set in. Not everyone was so forthcoming.

The insurance industry attracted a huge amount of bad publicity when they refused to pay out on property insurance claims.

'Act of God' they intoned, over and over.

2

So my family home and contents were gone, never to be replaced.

Thankfully, life insurance was a different matter. I realised I must have inherited my fatalistic streak from my Father. He had ensured that, in the event of my parents' untimely demise, any surviving offspring would be 'taken care of'.

And I was.

While undoubtedly a tragedy of epic proportions, there are always those ready to seize the opportunity to sweep away the ruins of the old and start anew.

Initially, there was widespread resistance to redevelopment. Many people wanted to have the area designated a huge memorial park.

However, due to the lack of residential and commercial land in the North of England, the builders won the day. They had already made a mark with the reconstruction of the Motorway network, transected by the explosion. It had been a vital link from North to South and even the staunchest memorialists could not oppose its reconnection.

So, over the next five years, from the flattened remains of Leeds rose the elegant form of Hope City.

The naming of the new city was the source of much controversy.

Some maintained that it should simply be called 'Leeds' in memory of the city it replaced.

Others argued that, whatever it might be, it would never be Leeds, so the name was rejected. 'New Leeds' was turned down, for the same reason.

A small group favoured a return to the Anglo-Saxon name of

'Loidis'. That was vetoed on the basis that it sounded too much like a bank. Likewise 'Nova Loidis' and 'Loidis Renatus' were spurned, for being too pretentious for Yorkshire Folk.

The committee charged with selecting a name were split over 'Phoenix'.

It was seriously considered, with its connotations of rebirth, but objectors pointed to possible confusion with the city in the USA.

Advocates argued that there was a 'Birmingham' in both countries and that 'We had York, centuries before they built New York' but the idea was dismissed.

Eventually, by a majority decision, the committee selected 'Hope City'.

A proposal to call it 'New Hope' was derailed by an elder statesman who warned of the possibility of the committee becoming embroiled in a copyright battle with the estate of the late film-maker George Lucas. Once the potential conflict had been explained to the younger members of the committee, the suggestion was withdrawn and 'Hope City' was officially adopted.

Well, that's the name on the maps. The locals christened it Crater City although, due to the lack of ground impact, there was actually never a crater.

The city was designed in concentric circles, with diverging spokes radiating out from the memorial that marked the approximate epicentre of the blast. Officially named the Hub, the locals referred to it as Ground Zero.

Ironically, as the wide pedestrian boulevards around the Hub gave way to the tighter packed rings of the outer residential areas, aerial photographs revealed an optical illusion. The centre of the city appeared as a dome. Or, perhaps, a crater. It depended on your perspective.

The lamentable loss of life had meant that the returning population was significantly smaller than the number of original inhabitants. The town planners took advantage of extra space to build in more green areas and reduce the overall height of the buildings in the city.

The idea was to get away from the high-rise city centre model, while still providing enough affordable homes to solve the housing shortage which plagued many other cities.

Bought with the proceeds of my Father's careful forward planning, I was to become the proud owner of a new two-bedroomed apartment in one of the green 'rings', close to the centre.

I'll admit, it took me a while to find my feet after my parents died.

For a start, I was pretty much homeless for several years, while the site of the calamity was cleared and redeveloped.

I spent some time with Uncles and cousins. I visited relations I hadn't seen in years.

I even took a couple of holidays in Europe.

My education pretty much came to an end, when my college was vaporised. Some schools, further afield, offered courses to the 'displaced' survivors of Leeds.

There weren't that many of us.

Some took the opportunities. I declined.

The fractured transport network made travel in the area difficult and I just couldn't raise the enthusiasm.

I tried to stay in contact with my peers but with little success. With most of them, I only had two things in common. One was college. The other was the Space Rock which destroyed college,

5

and everything else.

Besides, you can't stay friends with people you were never really friends with in the first place.

I attended the mandated counselling sessions and a couple of support group meetings. The raw expression of other people's crushing grief did nothing to ease my own. I stopped attending.

I guess I spent at least eighteen months living a kind of numb half-life. Survivor guilt can be debilitating. Guilt for not being able to save them. Guilt for not having spent more time with them. Guilt for the things I'd never said and done. And for the things I had.

Of all the stages of grieving, the hardest to get through was Denial. I'd seen the pictures of Leeds on the newscasts, but couldn't relate it to the city I'd lived in. I even tried ringing home, just in case someone would answer.

When Denial passed, Anger was confusing. I didn't know who to be angry with. A 10,000-ton meteor? The Americans? My parents? Myself, for being out of town? For a while, I was just angry at the world.

After that, I was too tired and numb to be depressed. Some of my ex-college mates were not so lucky. Suicide, drug and alcohol abuse and a gamut of mental health issues were recorded at alarming rates among the survivors.

I knew my parents would have wanted me to look forward and start planning my future. That's why they were so well insured.

Sadly I had absolutely no idea what I was going to do. The very idea of making plans, just so Fate could tear them to pieces again, was an anathema.

With no formal qualifications, job opportunities were limited. I worked in a number of fast-food outlets. I tried seasonal work in the agricultural industry. I even did a stint in construction but I'm not really built for outdoor grafting.

I was just drifting.

While I was working as a hospital porter, Luck took a hand again.

During a night shift, I was scanning the ads on the hospital intranet. The pay wasn't brilliant, and I was always on the lookout for extra little jobs to supplement it.

'Life models wanted for Art classes. Minimum Wage applies'

Well, I wasn't about to turn down money for sitting doing nothing. I noted the number and called it the next day.

Within a couple of weeks, I was posing in the centre of a circle of easels, dressed only in my speedos. Believe me, sitting absolutely still for forty-five minutes at a time is not as easy as it sounds.

I was managing to fit in two sessions a week at the Art College, around my hospital shifts, and was getting to know some of the tutors.

After about a month, one of the lecturers, Ray, asked "Have you ever done any photographic work?"

"As a model?"

"Yeah. I also teach photography. We don't do a lot of model work, but there is a module in the course on lighting and photographing for advertising. I could use a good looking guy, on a short-term basis."

He laughed at my expression "Hmm, that didn't come out right. Don't panic. I'm spoken for.

Could you manage an hour or two for the next three weeks?"

"I'll need to check my rota but, if you give me the dates and times, I can try to sort something out."

Luckily, I only needed to organise one shift swap to fit Ray's timetable and was soon stepping in front of the camera for the first time. This was completely different to art modelling.

No more holding a pose, to the point of cramp. I was changing posture and expression ten times a minute. It was great.

There was action and a buzz about the whole session. The ten students all took turns to prepare and shoot their sets, then went back to their workstations to download and edit their images.

I met up with Ray afterwards.

"How was it?" he asked.

"Brilliant. I loved it. I can't wait for the next session."

"Glad to hear it. Listen, if you really enjoyed it so much, what would you think of the idea of taking it up full-time?"

"Seriously? It's hardly a stable income."

"I know. It's a competitive field, but you shoot really well. I have a friend, Lauren Cooper, who is just starting her own agency and is looking for models. I'm sure she'd love to meet you. If it's OK, I'll send her some of the shots we've taken today, and see what she says."

"No harm in trying."

I met up with Lauren the next week and had my first professional shoot the week after that.

There was a lot to learn but most of her clients were new aspiring photographers who were also learning their craft and still treated their models with respect, like human beings, not window dummies. I found some of the most talented were often the most self-effacing.

My career went from strength to strength and I was soon able to quit the portering job.

Two years in, I broke into commercial videos.

When I was a kid, big advertisers used to pay extra to have

their ads aired at specific times of day. Things changed.

With most of the population now getting their entertainment fix streamed, at a time of their choosing, the whole idea of Prime Time was history. Advertisers now paid to place their ads in the breaks of specific shows, matched to viewer demographics.

Targeted advertising became the watchword. Quality over quantity. That meant that the advertisers were buying less airtime, so they had more money to spend on ad production. Some advertising campaigns had bigger budgets than the shows they interrupted.

I'd been pretty lucky. Lauren had managed to place me in some classy campaigns, and I was getting known as the Action Hero Spy Guy type.

She was angling to get me an actual acting role in an upcoming espionage mini-series.

That's when Fate decided it was time to take back with one hand what she had given me with the other.

2

Chapter 2

I suppose, in retrospect, I was lucky. Not everyone survives being thrown from a moving vehicle.

Conversely, the chances of a motor vehicle collision are lower now than at any time since the car was invented.

Very few people own and drive personal cars any more. During the past ten years, compensation culture, fed by the 'no win - no fee' mentality had bled the insurance companies dry. Their only recourse was to pass their losses on to drivers and increase premiums. This led to an increase in uninsured drivers, which led to more uninsured losses, more claims. It was a vicious cycle.

Convictions skyrocketed and using a car became even more expensive.

Successive Governments demonised the internal combustion engine. Diesel was the first to fall by the wayside. Then, as Electric Vehicles became the norm, petrol pumps began to disappear, and it became more and more difficult to continue to run a petrol-engined car.

The biggest problem with E-vehicles was the cost. Public transport struggled to cope with the increase in passengers, as private car ownership slumped.

The solution came in the form of Y-drive. Initially touted as 'Why Drive?', until the Marketing Department came up with a snappier name, it promised cheap and reliable 'almost personal' car use, at a fraction of the cost.

A multinational consortium threw their resources into producing autonomous, self-driving, on-your-doorstep electric taxis.

The Taxee was born.

The premise was simple. They eliminated the costs associated with private vehicles while offering an instantly available personal use vehicle.

The customers didn't have to worry about insurance, fuel costs, maintenance or driving under the influence of alcohol, or their recreational drug of choice.

With no drivers, fares were a fraction of those of traditional taxis which soon disappeared from the roads. That is, after a brief series of protests and attempts to sabotage the new vehicles. The majority of privately owned cars followed, soon after.

Most of the human-driven EVs left on the roads were owned by big business. They were mainly operated by companies whose employees actually drove enough miles to justify the investment.

Other organisations preferred that a third party not have a record of their staff's comings and goings, so ran their own vehicles.

In the main, they were status symbols, along with the uniformed chauffeurs who frequently drove them.

Some companies even kept bunkered stocks of petrol, to allow them to run limited fleets of internal combustion-powered cars. These were often sports cars and loaned to executives as perks of the job.

It was one such perk which put an end to my Secret Agent TV aspirations and, almost, my life.

I had been collected by an AI-driven EV to go to screen testing for the, as yet un-named, Secret Agent miniseries.

As we approached the outskirts of Hope City, I was reading the script in the back of the car.

A bright light in front of us caught my attention and I looked up. Heading directly towards us, at speed, was a red Porsche. It was on the wrong side of the road and, apparently, out of control. I checked my seatbelt was fastened and hung on to the armrest, waiting for the Autodriver to take evasive action.

It pulled hard to the left, but too late. The Porsche hit the Taxee on the offside and sent it spinning across an intersection. My script and coffee flew across the cab. Panic-stricken and disoriented, I felt as if I were on an out of control Roller Coaster.

I have no idea at what speed the Taxee hit the wall. All I know is that it was going backwards.

Everything seemed to happen in slow motion. I remember feeling detached as if watching someone else having an accident. My panic had subsided. I was resigned to the fact that Fate would play her hand, come what may.

My seatbelt, designed to restrain me in the event of a front-end collision, remained slack. As the impact buckled the rear of the Taxee, the front end lifted high into the air. With the back of my seat now almost horizontal, I slid easily up and out of my belt, exiting through the crazed remains of the rear windscreen.

Suddenly, time was running at its normal speed again. I was flying through the air. My face felt as if I'd been mauled by a wildcat. Just as panic began to take hold, I hit the wall. Everything went black.

The surgeons told me the scarring would fade but, from a professional standpoint, it was a simple case of "Forget the close-up. Mr. DeMille."

Surprise, surprise. Even in these enlightened times, the only acceptable cleft in the Good Guy's chin is the one put there by Mother Nature. You see, it all comes down to merchandising. What's the point of creating an Action Hero, if you can't then sell him to the aftershave and skin care advertisers afterwards?

That's not to say work dried up altogether, but there was limited demand for scar-faced villains, and little more for guys with beards.

After my parents' Life Insurance Policy paid out, it appears the Insurance Industry decided I'd taken enough from their coffers.

Although enough to put the brakes on my acting aspirations, my facial scarring was assessed as 'minor'. My top lip carried a scar which looked as if I'd had a childhood cleft palate repair. Although my lips had healed without a visible mark, the scar continued downward from just below my mouth, across to the left of my chin. From a few feet away, they were hardly visible.

To the camera, it was a different matter. They showed up like fresh weals.

As I hadn't yet signed a contract on the miniseries, I couldn't even claim for future loss of earnings.

I received a derisory sum, in consideration of 'psychological trauma'. It covered the bills during the healing period and left with me with a small remainder to invest in my future.

During my photographic modelling career, I'd taken an interest in the technical aspects of photography. To the despair of my erstwhile employer, Ray, I'd never shown any flair for the artistic side of camerawork.

13

Nonetheless, I sought him out and booked a course in industrial photography. Realism suited my temperament better than creativity.

With a recognised qualification under my belt, what my Mother would have called 'something to fall back on', I began looking for work.

Acting roles are limited for anyone with facial disfigurement. Photographic modelling jobs just don't exist.

That's how I came to be employed as a freelance Crime Scene Recorder.

Much as car dashcams became almost obligatory, before owner-driving became a thing of the past, so wearcams were the must-have accessory of the late 20's.

The technology initially sprang from the growing popularity for turning one's whole life into an online Soap Opera. Coincidentally wearcams became a significant crime-solving tool.

Hidden in glasses or a piece of jewellery, a button or a cap, access to a recording of a crime, from the victim's point of view was invaluable.

Unlike early versions, later wearcams instantly uploaded their footage to the owner's online storage. They could decide what they wanted to share, after reviewing the day's recording.

Police and security services had access to the storage Servers and could pull footage, even if the camera was destroyed or stolen. Needless to say, those involved in dubious activities tended not to wear them.

Judges could now view recordings of the crimes defendants were accused of. The investigation workload of Police Forces dwindled. So too did the need to employ specialist Crime Scene Investigation Units.

With budgets cut, most Police Forces outsourced the work of

photography and sample collection. That's where I came in. The hours were unsocial, but the pay was generous. Since I'd lost my family, I'd tended to avoid personal attachments, so I could hardly be described as sociable, myself. The job suited me.

I barely heard the vibrating of my phone over the sound of the coffee maker. I was the on-call Scene Recorder, and Dispatch had a job. I pressed the 'Accept' button in the Secure App and accessed the details.

I grabbed my holocam and launched the Taxee app on my phone.

I had no idea what the job would entail but, typically, work varied from vehicle collisions to cataloging a victim's injuries to actual scenes of homicide.

The cab arrived three minutes later, pulled up soundlessly to the kerb and my phone bleeped to announce its arrival.

Displaying the QR code on the phone screen to the cab's door scanner resulted in the usual 'door opening' warning, and the side of the cab slid open.

Inside was relatively clean. As the location of all pickups was electronically archived, and the interior of the saloon was under constant surveillance, the Taxees were rarely targets of vandalism, of the interior anyhow. As passengers' credit details were stored in the App before you could hail a cab, it was a simple matter for the company to reclaim the cost of any reparations, in the case of malicious damage.

The Taxee AI already had my destination so, once my seatbelt was fastened, it accelerated silently into the traffic.

According to the infopanel, the journey should take about 15 minutes so, ignoring the video ads on the interior display, I slipped on my vGlasses to check for any more messages, and catch up on the news.

3

Chapter 3

The street was full of large upmarket houses, and armed Police. Flashing blue lights reflected off 'do not enter' tape. My I.D. card got me by the tape, a policeman with a scanner recording my entry and verifying my identity. Asking for the Scene Officer, I was directed up the steps.

The number of guns on display made me nervous. My curiosity was aroused by the shattered remains of the wooden front door hanging between carved stone pillars.

This didn't look like any crime scene I'd worked before. The exterior and interior doors looked as if they had been hit with a battering ram.

I passed through, and down the hall. The expensive carpet was covered in boot prints. Most appeared to be mud. Some looked like blood.

Displaying the I.D. again and repeating my enquiry, I followed directions through to the lounge at the rear.

When you hear the word 'bloodbath', there's always the association with the word 'bath' that makes you think of a contained body of liquid.

When you actually see one, you realise that 'bloodshower'

would be a more appropriate term.

The neatly arranged lounge, with its period furniture, looked as if someone had swung a large bucket in an arc, drenching most of the floor, and three of the walls. There was a metallic taste in the air, and I wondered how so much fluid could come from one person. As the armed policeman guarding the doorway stepped aside, my question was answered. I gagged, and stepped back, hard into the wall behind me, struggling to master my last meal.

I'd photographed a few bodies before. Death by stabbing or gunshot was not commonplace in Hope City, but I'd seen my share. That could not have prepared me for the carnage before me.

I struggled to imagine what weapon might be capable of reducing a human body to such a state.

In fact, I was struggling to identify the remains as human.

Entrails and strips of flesh spread across the carpet. A larger concentration of flesh could have been the torso, but even bones had been reduced to such splinters that it was hard to guess.

I had a grotesque mental image of a person being fed into a wood-chipper. That would have the same effect, but there was no way anyone had sneaked large arboricultural machinery into the house.

Feeling rather foolish, I glanced up at the ceiling, half expecting to see linear splatter marks, from the use of a chainsaw. Wrong again.

Well, my job was to simply record the scene and leave the interpretation to the experts.

I fumbled for my I.D. showed it to the Officer in charge who glanced briefly and nodded grimly for me to begin working.

I assembled my projector, casting a red laser matrix on the

floor and walls, and began to record each area with the holo-cam.

I had to work carefully so as not to disturb evidence which is not easy when the room is carpeted with it.

I already had almost a dozen shots and was alone in the room. A quiet cough interrupted my concentration.

The man standing behind me would be about my age, with short black hair, swept back from a slightly receding hairline. Dark brown eyes studied me from beneath thick, but neat, black eyebrows. He waited, his hands in the pockets of his smart grey raincoat, open at the front to reveal an expensive looking suit.

"Yes?"

"You may go now, thank you. We will be taking over the scene and the recording of all evidence"

I was struck by his accent. He spoke like the King. With his long rounded vowels and precisely enunciated consonants. The Spy show I had aspired to star in had several characters who affected the same accent.

For an actor, it's a nightmare. Unless you're born to it, it can be very difficult to carry off. Fail, and you end up sounding like what we used to call an 'Upper-Class Twit'. Sadly that's exactly what happened to the show.

Widely condemned by critics but loved by the Americans, who couldn't hear the difference, it only lasted one season.

He didn't sound like a policeman.

"We?"

He produced a card from the inside pocket of his jacket and held it up to eye level. It bore a large V-shaped logo, and holo-image of its holder, and his name.

Vanguard - Field Supervisor: R.Simons.

"Vanguard? Never heard of it."

"Unsurprising, but you'll find that the Officer in charge has surrendered the scene to us, which means that I now control the investigation. My colleague will escort you from the premises." He called back over his shoulder "Walters."

Footsteps sounded along the hallway, in answer to his call and another raincoat-clad man entered.

Seeing me in my white all-in-one, his face was a mask of surprise.

"Nube?"

"Xander?"

Simons' consternation was clear

"You know each other?"

His newly-arrived colleague nodded affirmatively

"Supervisor Simons, may I introduce you to Jack Allman, AKA Nube, also known as Skarvak the vile, space pirate and pretender to the Kalifat of Ansoria."

I cringed at the mention of one of my least favourite acting roles

"Jesus, Xander. You actually watched that?"

"Let's just say I have a nephew with very poor taste in TV."

"Nephew? You mean little Angie...?"

"Angela's got two now. The youngest is a girl,Tara. Times move on, Nube"

Simons coughed again, less politely this time.

"Gentlemen, if we could please wind up the reunion, we have work to do"

With a twinge of guilt, I recalled that the last time I'd seen Alexander Walters had been at the Leeds Memorial Service. That was before they broke ground on the new City. The scene of a brutal slaying wasn't an ideal location to try and catch up.

He carefully placed the briefcase he was carrying on a relatively clear patch of carpet.

"Sorry, Sir. Haven't seen each other in quite a while." He looked up at me "Watch closely, Nube. You'll love this, even though it will eventually put you out of a job."

He opened the case fully and, from recesses in the base and the lid, removed a number of mini-drones. A screen in the case illuminated and, with a couple of quick swipes, he started the drones' motors. They rose quickly into the air and began to circulate around the room.

"Right, let's leave them to their work"

As I followed him and Simons out of the room he continued his explanation.

"Autonomous recording drones, with 3D cameras. They will map and record everything in the room, saving it to a central server.

When you want to review the scene you're no longer limited to holo-images. You can slip on your vGlasses and explore a complete 3D VR Render of the location, overlaying measurements where required. Plus they scan in InfraRed and UV"

"Mr Allman. Walters and I have a little more information to gather from the local police, while his toys do their work but I will need to speak with you again shortly, before you leave. This scene is, shall we say, sensitive, and I'll need to ensure that all images you recorded are securely erased to prevent potential information leakage."

"Well, I..."

"Thank you, Mr Allman"

He spun on his heel and walked off.

I opened the wrought iron gate and strode down the passage between the houses, towards the garden at the rear.

I was gritting my teeth in irritation at Simons' suggestion that I might breach scene confidentiality. Did he think he was dealing with an amateur?

Then I stopped and laughed. Perhaps Xander's theatrical introduction of his friend, the B-movie villain actor, had slightly undermined my professional image.

With my back turned to the street, the lights atop the remaining police cars lit the darkened garden at the far end with a blue strobe effect.

The iron bench and the neat pebbled path leapt out of the darkness in pin-sharp clarity, every half a second.

The image was so intense, but monochromatic. It reminded me of a 1930's horror film, right down to the yellow eyes, blinking at me from behind the ornamental bush in the corner.

Whoa, back up! I shook my head, to try and clear it. Yellow eyes?

I was losing it for sure. I know I'd been pretty traumatised by the carnage in the house, but that was no need to let my imagination run riot.

I looked again. Nothing. Nonetheless, I felt the hairs on the back of my neck start to rise. I turned my back on the garden and was heading back to the street to wait for Simons when there was a rustling in the bushes. I froze. Had I really heard it?

I spun around and took a step back towards the bench. There. I could just make out a shape in the shadows at the bottom of the garden.

The eyes blinked again, looking straight at me. The shrubbery moved, as the eyes came closer. There was a rumble, like distant thunder. I realised it was a growl.

Before I had even begun to turn my head, to call over my shoulder for help from the gun-wielding police in their bullet-proof vests and riot helmets, I knew I wasn't going to make it.

In what seemed like a fraction of a second something grabbed me by the throat. Its grip was so tight I couldn't even breathe. I could taste my own blood. I could feel it running down the front of my shirt, mixing with the saliva dripping from the hairy jaws which were cutting off my supply of air.

I knew I was going to die. There would be no 'pick yourself up, dust yourself off and start all over again' this time.

I clawed at the giant muzzle and tried to pull it off my throat, but its grip was so secure that I only caused myself more pain.

I could see one yellow eye in front of my face, growing dimmer as I tried to focus. There was no more growling, just the quiet of the otherwise deserted garden and the ragged, vile-smelling panting of the beast.

It seemed determined to end my life before I could reveal its presence. I wondered if this were the animal responsible for the slaughter in the house. Hot tears ran down my cheeks as I beat the creature feebly about the head. I knew that once I lost consciousness, I would never regain it.

"Mr Allman?"

The sound of Simons' voice stirred me to a final futile struggle. I kicked the animal's body and tried to force a cry from my bursting lungs. Its teeth clenched tighter around my throat as if it knew I could give it away.

Then there was a shot. The animal recoiled but did not release its grip.

"Jesus Christ!" Simons' voice

Another shot. Another, and the sound of approaching boots.

The clamp around my throat suddenly released, and I slid down the wall. My head was spinning and my throat burned as I fought to fill my lungs.

A grey hairy mass stood over me. It was bigger than the largest Rottweiler I've ever seen. Huge yellow eyes reflected the light of the approaching torches.

I couldn't look away. Guns fired again, and the beast turned towards the approaching police, snarling.

With a final look at my face, it retreated towards the bottom of the garden, vaulted effortlessly over the fence, and disappeared into the night.

My last conscious sensation was one of surprise. When it turned to look at me, I had expected to see nothing but feral savagery on its face. Instead, as my sight failed, I was convinced I saw an expression of deep sorrow, even regret, in those huge yellow eyes. I was still debating with myself whether it was an illusion, caused by lack of oxygen, when I finally succumbed to my injuries and passed out.

4

Chapter 4

I dreamed of blood.

I saw the murder scene again, like a sepia photograph, but tinted red, instead of yellow. There was no trace of the victim's remains, but the blood had pooled on the rug, coagulating into the tassels along the edge.

My attention was drawn to the arcs of gore, splashed across the embossed wallpaper, as if with a giant paintbrush. The blood had run down the wall, under some of the crescents, making a pattern like an ornate hair comb.

I could smell the tang of iron in the air. I was appalled, not by the blood, but by my own strange fascination with it. Was blood always such a rich deep red?

Reaching out, I traced shapes in the wetness on the coffee table. It was cold, and slightly sticky, dripping from my fingers, as I raised them towards my face. It smelled sweet. Savouring the aroma, I opened my mouth.

What the hell was I doing? I recoiled in disgust, lurching backwards from the shining pools which tried to draw me in.

Something underfoot moved, and I tripped, falling into the red, congealing mass. It suddenly seemed so deep, as it rose up and threatened to engulf me. I began to sink.

Now the blood was warm. It was life. I needed it. I wanted to be absorbed by it.

Then I heard the growl.

5

Chapter 5

My eyes snapped open. The bloody room was gone. I didn't recognise my surroundings. I was in a bed. The mattress was soft but there was a powerful smell of antiseptic. A hospital?

I took a deep breath. I was alive. I didn't know whether to laugh or cry.

The walls of the room were white. The bright light reflecting from them seemed harsh to eyes just open from sleep. A door opened into a curved corridor, which I could see through a small window beside the bed. Another looked as if it were either a cupboard or, perhaps, an en-suite.

I had an infusion running into my left arm. Under my hospital gown, I could feel electrodes stuck to my chest. My vital signs were displaying on a wall screen at the side of the bed.

Furniture was sparse, an overbed table, a trolley across the room, a bedside locker and an armchair in one corner.

The armchair was the source of the sound I had mistaken for growling. I recognised the snoring man as the Vanguard Supervisor, Simons.

In sleep, he looked far less domineering than he had been when I had first encountered him at the scene of the killing. His smart suit was the worse for him sleeping in it and his previously clean-shaven face showed at least a couple of days of stubble.

A couple of days? How long had I been asleep? Asleep...the sudden recollection of my last conscious moments flooded back, and I involuntarily cried out, clutching at my throat.

Disturbed by my outcry, Simons stirred, rubbing his eyes. When he managed to focus on me he rose quickly from the chair and crossed to the side of the bed. I caught a strong odour of garlic from his breath. There was an unfortunate body odour too. I wondered how long he had been in that chair.

"Welcome back, Mr Allman. We were beginning to wonder if you'd ever wake up. We've been taking it in turns keeping an eye on you. Walters will be delighted to hear that you have decided to grace us with your presence once more."

"What?" I stammered, "Where?"

"Easy, old chap. All in good time. You've had a rough ride, and still have some recovering to do."

I wondered if he was beginning to doubt my ability to form complete sentences, based on our previous brief conversation, and my current difficulty communicating, so I took a deep breath and asked

"Where am I?"

"A little private facility we use to treat ah, 'recuperating' Agents when we don't want to have to answer too many questions about the cause of their injuries."

"Did you catch it?"

Simons brushed his hand back over his scalp smoothing down a few unruly hairs. He sighed deeply. "Unfortunately, no. I know I hit it, at least twice but once it was over the fence it was gone. We didn't find a trace."

"How long have I, you..." coherent speech escaped me again,

but Simons took my meaning.

"It's been an uphill struggle. You lost a lot of blood, and suffered some awful injuries." My hand strayed to my throat again."You healed very quickly, surprised the Doctors, but you've been unconscious quite a while"

"A while?"

"A couple of weeks." he winced at my expression.

"As I said, the wounds healed quickly, but there was a problem with infection. At first, they thought you might have contracted rabies. It was pretty nasty, watching them shoving that horse syringe into your abdomen but, apparently, that's the most effective treatment."

Lifting the front of the hospital gown, I examined my belly, but there was no sign of puncture marks.

"Then they worried it could be MRSA, so they pumped you full of antibiotics. Your fever just wouldn't break. You were thrashing around, frothing at the mouth. You almost looked like a mad dog yourself. Finally, they decided it was a viral infection, and tried a cocktail of drugs, most of which I've never even heard of. Must have done the trick, though. How do you feel?"

I paused for a moment to consider my response. The answer surprised me. I felt as if I had just woken from a long relaxing sleep. I had no aches or pains, felt alert and energised. I swung my legs around and sat on the edge of the bed.

"Now hold on." Simons cautioned "Not until the Doctor's had a look at you and, before you go anywhere, we need to have a serious chat about what happened, and how you're going to tell it to anyone who asks." That sounded ominous.

Pressing the call button, Simons excused himself, promising to return later. He had no sooner left the room than the Doctor arrived. She was definitely not what I expected.

Her name badge identified her as Doctor Anthea Dixon. It was pinned to the left lapel of a tailored blue suit jacket which covered a mandarin-collared white silk blouse. The matching skirt fell to just below her knees, and her almost flat leather shoes completed the ensemble. Her dark brown hair was pulled back into a neat bun, a few strands left loose to frame her face.

She smelled of honeysuckle. I closed my eyes and inhaled.

"Agent Allman?"

My attention returned to her face, where a pair of baby blue eyes regarded me quizzically from behind a pair of frameless designer glasses.

"Agent? are you feeling alright?"

"Sorry. Yes, but it's not 'Agent'. It's just 'Mr'. Just Jack"

"Jack, then. I'm glad to see you've finally woken up. I'm Doctor Dixon. You may not know it, but you've given us a few sleepless nights over the last three weeks."

"Three weeks? I thought it was only a fortnight?"

She smiled "Supervisor Simons probably understated the length of your recovery to avoid distressing you. I think he holds himself partially responsible for your misfortune. Actually, he probably saved your life. It was he who fought off whatever it was that attacked you"

"Whatever? I assumed it was a dog."

I looked away, trying to form an image in my mind, All I could see were the yellow eyes.

"That has been a matter of some debate." she continued " While your neck wounds closely resembled damage caused by canine dentition, there were claw marks on your chest which were more reminiscent of big cat or bear attacks"

My memory rewound to the scene of the attack, where I'd first met Simons. Funny, I couldn't even remember being clawed.

Having an animal's jaw clamped around your throat tends to make you immune to such distractions.

"So which was it?"

"I really couldn't say. The animal escaped and has evaded capture. I believe all local zoos and collectors of exotic animals were interviewed, but no-one admits to having 'mislaid' any specimens" She smiled again.

"So what happens now?" I asked.

"Well, your physical injuries have healed remarkably quickly, and with no scarring, thanks to some excellent work by our surgical team, but we'd like to keep you here for a few days more, for rehabilitation. Supervisor Simons also has to debrief you."

She pursed her lips disapprovingly at my raised eyebrow.

"Surely you're in no rush to get back to that empty apartment? You've been on full Crime Scene Recorder pay ever since the incident. Your CSR agency has been informed, as has your um, Theatrical Agent." She stifled a smile "And the sooner you leave here, the sooner you have to return to work"

I wasn't surprised that she knew I lived alone. Employees of the security services do have to sacrifice a certain amount of personal privacy. It goes with the employment.

"I've already notified the kitchen that you're awake. I'm sure you'll be hungry. After you've eaten, Supervisor Simons will be back to see you, then we'll have the Physiotherapist start you on some gentle exercises. You'd be surprised how quickly muscles can atrophy when they're not used regularly. I'll see you again later"

As she exited the door, which swung both ways like the entrance to a western saloon, I caught a whiff of food cooking and almost began to salivate. Hungry? What an understatement.

Lunch was pretty good. Roast beef with garlic mash and green vegetables. Definitely not standard hospital canteen fare. I thought the cook had been a little overfond of the salt and would have preferred the beef a little rarer, but I'd paid for worse in restaurants. Maybe that was just a reflection on my choice of restaurant.

I'd devoured a dish of apple tart and ice-cream, but refused the cheese and biscuits, when Simons returned. He'd shaved and changed his shirt. He must have showered too, as the unpleasant odour was absent. A mint mouthwash almost masked the smell of garlic.

"Mr Allman. Looking better and better"

"Thanks. By the way, it's Jack"

"Jack. Very good. Listen, I don't know if you even remember, but I wanted to apologise, for that night. You know."

"You want to apologise for saving my life?"

"Good heavens, no...I.."

He looked up and caught me grinning.

"Ah, humour. No. What I meant to say was that I may have appeared a little rude. We were in the middle of a 'sensitive' situation, to which you should not have been given access. Local Dispatch knew we were en route and should never have allocated the job to you. I wasn't miffed at you, personally. I fear I may have neglected to afford you an appropriate level of professional courtesy. You just happened to be in the firing line.."

"In more ways than one."

He rubbed the back of his neck, with his left hand, as if trying to ease a crick.

"Indeed. We need to talk about that."

"What the hell was it ?"

"A panther, being used by a local photographer, got spooked

32

by the flashgun and escaped. It was recaptured and has been destroyed. It would seem the fashion models weren't too keen on sharing a set with it again."

"But Doctor Dixon said .. Wait a minute.. that's bullshit. You're feeding me a press release."

"Doctor Dixon should know better"

He didn't hide his annoyance well.

His officious attitude reasserted itself.

"Listen. To be honest, we have no hard evidence what attacked you, but it's not expedient to admit that to the press. You agreed to certain conditions when you signed up to work with the police. Confidentiality was one of them. All we're doing, with this story, is helping you to maintain plausible deniability."

"But I don't know anything"

"And that is the way it will stay. One more thing. You never entered the house, and you definitely never saw what had happened in the lounge."

"Like I'll be able to forget that in a hurry."

"Well, apart from the physical therapy, we have that covered too. You'll be attending counselling sessions once a week on your release."

"No, I'll be fine."

"It's not optional. But it is paid."

He grinned, more relaxed.

"Well, best get back to work. Just one thing. Did you see anyone else in the garden before you were attacked?"

I searched my memory. "No. Why?"

"Just a line of enquiry. In case the animal had a handler."

"Are you saying this wasn't a random animal attack?"

"No jumping to conclusions please, Mr. Allman. It's a routine question. As far as that goes, I know as much as you, which is nothing. Agreed?"

I nodded.

"Very well. Here's my card. If you remember anything else about what happened in the garden, please do let me know. Get well soon, Jack."

Sam, the physio wasn't exactly a bundle of laughs. He stood about six feet two and must have weighed almost three hundred pounds. With his shaven head, he looked like he'd been chiseled out of granite, then dropped into one or two rugby scrums for a little realignment of his facial features. He was surprisingly careful when he lifted me out of bed and placed me in a wheelchair, but predictably forceful when I protested.

"It's for your own good, Jack."

I wasn't about to get into an argument with the man-mountain so I kept quiet as he wheeled me down the blank white corridor.

It was the first time I'd been out of my room unless you counted assisted visits to the en-suite bathroom. I kept telling the nurses I was fine, but they insisted on frog marching me to the toilet, one either side. They did, at least, release me and allow me to close the door, once inside.

The corridor, like my room, was lit with low-energy bulbs, set into frosted glass uplighters, instead of the fluorescents I'd expect to see in a public hospital. I had yet to see a window, and no-one had mentioned anything about the location of the 'facility' as Simons had delicately described it. There was little to see in the corridor, just more darkened windows which gave a view into empty cubicles, either side. It appeared I was the only patient. A nurse sat at a desk, in an alcove, about ten feet from my door, on the inner side of the curve. The wall screen beside her showed views into the empty rooms, mine included.

"Mind the feet."

Sam used the footplates of the wheelchair to push open one of a set of double doors leading into a room on the left. It was more brightly-lit than the corridor. The walls were adorned with charts showing the human skeleton and the location and names of the larger muscle groups, along with other detailed close-up anatomical diagrams. There was a desk on the left of the room, under the window which showed the corridor outside. It held a tablet, a telephone and an articulated scale-model of the spine. Most of the floor was bare woodgrain laminate, or perhaps wood. I couldn't really tell, but there was an exercise mat rolled out opposite the desk. Beside it were a pair of waist-high parallel bars which ran halfway down the room. Racked in one corner were weights, arranged by size. A small multigym and a pyramid of three steps with a handrail stood in the opposite corner. A padded treatment couch completed the equipment.

Positioning the chair between the parallel bars, Sam offered a hand. My own looked lost in his huge palm, as I took it, and placed my other on one of the bars.

"You may prefer to push up from the chair with that hand, rather than pulling." he suggested. Feeling pretty stupid, sitting there holding the hand of Hercules, I meekly complied, just wanting to get the show over with. To be honest, since I'd woken up, I'd been feeling fine, better than fine. Apart from a slight burning sensation around my throat, I couldn't remember when I'd felt better.

"O.K. easy .. up"

I did as instructed. This time it was Sam's turn to feel foolish, as I simply stepped out of the chair and stood, solid and unaided, but still holding his hand. He looked me up and down, then released his grip.

"O.K. good. Now take a few steps."

I felt like I was back in the shoe shop where my mother used to take me at the end of each summer holiday, as Sam watched me promenade up and down between the bars.

For the next ten minutes or so, I demonstrated what I had learned up to the age of two. Stand up, sit down, climb the stairs, lean forward, touch your toes. Sam seemed genuinely surprised at my ability to retain my balance when he tried pushing me first from the left, then right, front, then back.

"Pretty good shape. Do you work out?"

"In your dreams."

"Hmm. Let's finish with some weights"

With a mischievous smile, he led me to the rack. His biceps swelled as he hefted a couple and held them out to me.

"Try these for size."

I tensed, waiting for the weight when he released, but instead, my arms moved upwards, involuntarily, in anticipation of the downward pull that never came. I laughed.

"Good one, Sam. They look real."

Eyes wide with surprise, but apparently determined to carry on the charade, Sam took the weights from me, feigning effort as he replaced them on the rack. Wordlessly, he indicated the chair. I raised a questioning eyebrow and he shrugged and opened the door for me to walk back down the corridor to my room, without assistance.

Dinner was of the same standard as lunch. If I stayed here much longer, I could see me gaining some excess weight pretty quickly. Perhaps Sam's idea about working out wasn't such a bad one.

The nurse who fetched the meal asked if I would like anything to read and provided a tablet which had subscriber login to the daily news channels. It also had unlimited access to the latest movies, some of which I hadn't seen.

Later, as I began to contemplate sleep, it suddenly occurred to me that I actually had no idea what time it was. The Nurse reassured me that it was almost 11 pm, but I still felt unsettled as I turned out the lamp.

With the room illuminated only by a slight glow through the blinds covering the window on to the corridor, it also crossed my mind that this was probably the first time I'd been alone in the dark since the attack.

6

Chapter 6

My dreams were scarlet again.

I revisited the scene of the attack. I could almost hear the soft dripping of the blood as it ran down the tasselled lampshade and fell to the floor. The smell was more intense in my dream than it had been in reality, making my nostrils twitch and dilate.

The room was unoccupied. It was lit only by a single shaded bulb, which cast a cone below it, like a spotlight. The rest of the room was shrouded in darkness. Unlike my previous nightmare, the body, or what was left of it, was still there.

With the unnatural clarity of a dream, I dispassionately examined the remains, trying to determine where each ravaged part should connect to the next. Engrossed in my macabre jigsaw, I became aware that I was being watched.

In a shadowed corner of the room, a darker shape stirred. Familiar yellow eyes regarded me intensely. I didn't feel threatened, just curious to see what they belonged to.

I stood and turned towards the corner. The eyes retreated into the darkness, which echoed with a visceral growl.

Ignoring the warning, I took a step towards the shadows. As punishment for my bravado, a huge hairy mass burst into the light, too fast for me to focus clearly, and those razor-sharp fangs found my throat again.

This time I could feel the claws raking across my chest as I fought to free myself. Despite my struggles, the jaws did not tighten, and I realised that I was in no immediate danger.

With the beast's muzzle forcing my head back, I was unable to look down and see it clearly, but I had an impression of silver fur and immense bulk. As I resigned myself to whatever Fate had in store, I was overcome with a sense of peace.

I stopped struggling. I closed my eyes and relaxed in the creature's grip. I felt no pain as it began to move, walking at first, then running, leaping, carrying me like a living ragdoll in its titanic jaws.

On it ran, and on, and I bounced and shook, and shook, and shook.

7

Chapter 7

I awoke to find Xander, with his hand on my shoulder, shaking me.

"Nube. Come on, Jack. Wake up. You were dreaming."

Blinking, the memory of my bizarre encounter fading from my mind, I asked

"What time is it?"

"It's a little after nine. I thought you might be ready for breakfast. Do you have any preference?"

"Steak, rare, with eggs and fries"

"Seriously, Buddy? This isn't the Hilton, you know. Here, put these on, and we'll take a stroll down to the canteen, and see what we can rustle up."

He passed me a two-piece sweat suit and I ducked into the en-suite to change.

Apart from my visit with Sam, the physio, I hadn't been out of my room.

This time we walked the opposite way along the corridor. A door on the left, at the end, opened into a semicircular space dotted with low tables and padded armchairs.

Several agents sat around in groups and pairs. Most were just chatting, coffee cups in hand. One or two had documents open on the tables.

It looked like an informal common area, rather than a meeting room. The walls were decorated with abstract framed art. A pyramidal wooden planter sat roughly in the centre of the space, plants cascading down its sides.

The atmosphere reminded me of a public plaza but, like the rest of the Vanguard facility I had seen, there were no windows. Everything was lit by LED bulbs, but these had been toned to give a softer, more yellow, hue than the clinical area.

At the midpoint of the long straight wall which formed the diameter of the semicircle, was a lift shaft. Glass doors either side led into the canteen.

Passing through, I found myself in a mirror-image of the room I had just left.

Circular tables were surrounded with high-backed chairs, giving the impression of a bistro, rather than a workplace canteen.

In the space occupied by the planter in the previous room stood the Robochef station.

Xander called up the menu on screen and selected two full English breakfasts, with coffee. The console spat out his numbered ticket and we retired to a table, leaving the mechanical cook to prepare our order.

"So, lucky escape, Buddy." he opened.

"So I'm told. Thankfully, I slept through it."

"Have to admit, I was getting worried you wouldn't make it. I had the impression, at one point, they'd pretty much given up hope. But then you suddenly turned the corner and...well, here we are."

I looked around at the Agents, occupied with their food.

"So where is 'here', exactly?"

"Ah. I'm sure that Simons will fill you in when he's ready."

I didn't press the matter. The Xander I remembered was never so evasive, but it had been a few years since we last met. It was at the Memorial Service after the disaster. Xander lost an older brother in the 'Event', as it was euphemistically labelled. He and the rest of his family had been in Europe on holiday. Although they lost everything, they were counted Survivors.

We spoke, instead of how our paths had diverged. He had joined the Navy. He saw it as a new start, to draw a line between the past and future.

He worked in telephony and radio. At some point, he started to handle encrypted communiques and that had led, eventually, to a spell working in Intelligence.

"And then I was recruited to work for Vanguard. " he concluded.

"Makes my patchwork quilt of an employment history look rather boring. " I admitted. "What do you actually do?"

"Well, I can't really go into too much detail, Buddy. Otherwise, I'd have to kill you afterwards. " He winked, but I wasn't altogether convinced that he was joking.

The Robochef announced the number on Xander's ticket, and we collected our food.

We continued our catch-up. I asked Xander about his sister and her family. Discussing the mundane made for a more relaxed conversation, but I still felt a little uneasy. It just felt incongruous to be talking about the banalities of family life, when I had recently woken up from a life-threatening attack by an unidentified animal.

More, I was eating breakfast in a windowless building, with no idea of where I was. For all I knew, the world had ended, for real this time, and we were in some underground bunker. I began to feel a little claustrophobic.

"She always had a crush on you, you know." Smiled Xander.

"Sorry?" I'd lost the thread.

"Angela. You'd be surprised how much her husband looks like you. And I swear she encouraged little Ross to watch that crappy Space Opera just so she could lust after the villain."

"Please, Xander. I just narrowly avoided being mauled to death by a wild beast. Now you want me to get beaten to a pulp by a jealous husband?"

He laughed.

We reminisced for a while. We had been pretty close at school, two geeks against the world. Now even his voice sounded strange to me. His Leeds accent had been moderated by that non-geographic inflection common to people who spend several years in His Majesty's Armed Forces. They all sound as if they hail from the same place, but you can't quite put your finger on where it might be.

Finally, he looked at his watch and pushed back his chair. "Better be getting you back. I had to get permission from Dixie to bring you out. She'll go mental if she goes to check up on you, and you're awol."

"Dixie?" I smirked "Really?"

"C'mon, Nube. You know how it is. I've known Doc Dixon a few years, and she's had to patch me up more than once. This body, with the shirt off. You get the picture? Anyhow, let's go, Buddy. Back to bed."

Doctor Dixon didn't come to see me that day.

The nurses called in every few hours, to take observations and mark my chart, but I was beginning to feel like a fraud.

Sam, the Physio had reported that he could find no signs of muscular deterioration but offered the use of his multigym, if I felt like a workout.

I declined.

Agent Simons paid me another visit, to enquire if I had remembered anything else of relevance, and to assure me that Vanguard was continuing its investigation into the attacks. I was realistic enough not to expect an early outcome.

That night was dreamless.

The next morning, I had showered and put the sweatsuit back on when there was a knock at the door. I could smell her perfume before she entered the room.

"Good morning, Jack. How are you feeling?"

For some reason, I had an overwhelming urge to respond with something cheesey like 'Better for seeing you.', but I fought the bizarre impulse and settled for "Very well. Thank you, Doctor. How are you?"

I might have been imagining it, but I swear I saw a slight flush in her cheek, in response to my question.

She continued "We're very pleased with your progress. The physiotherapist reports you fit, physically. How have you been sleeping?"

"I slept like a baby, last night." I neglected to mention the previous night. I didn't want to delay getting home any longer than necessary.

I'd had my share of therapy sessions following the death of my parents and was not about to volunteer for additional psychoanalysis if I could get away with it.

The Doctor consulted her notes and nodded. "Very well. I see no benefit in extending your stay. I'll talk to Supervisory Agent Simons and arrange your transport home. I'm giving you a sick note for a couple of weeks' recuperation. Oh, and here's the address of the Therapist you'll be seeing."

"That's really not necessary."

"The sessions have already been booked. We mandate post-trauma counselling for all our field Agents, so you're in good company. You may even find it helps."

She smiled, making a final entry on her tablet. "So, unless there's anything else you'd like to ask, I'll process your discharge."

I couldn't help myself. I had to ask. "How about your telephone number?"

This time she definitely blushed. She pushed her glasses up her nose with one finger.

"That's very flattering, Mr Allman. I'm not sure Supervisor Simons would consider it appropriate, however." She turned and headed for the door. On the threshold, she stopped "By the way, Agent Walters asked me to tell you that he is waiting for you in the canteen. Enjoy your breakfast, Jack." Smiling, she left.

I found my own way to the canteen and breakfasted with Xander.

We exited the area on the opposite side and took a short walk down the corridor to Simons' office.

He shook my hand, wished me well and ensured I was clear on the Vanguard version of events, should anyone ask. He confirmed I had the counsellor's address and that I would be contacted to arrange my first session.

I thanked him, once again, for the hospitality and for saving my life.

Xander waited in the corridor. He led the way back to the central lift and we ascended.

When we exited the lift, we were in a parking structure, apparently underground. I wondered how far below the surface my room had been.

He led me to a waiting vehicle. Obviously, Vanguard had its own private motor pool.

We sat in the back of a windowless van which served as Vanguard's private ambulance. There was a small window in the bulkhead which separated us from the human driver. From my seat, it was too small to get a clear view of the outside, so I had no idea of our location, or the route we took. After a month in Vanguard, I could not have found my way back, if I had wanted to.

Xander was quite animated.

"I know it's awkward, with my work, but we've got to try not to lose touch this time round. I'm sure Angie would like to catch up. " he winked, and I ignored it.

I studied his face, comparing it to my schoolboy recollections.

It was still round, with deep-set eyes. Years earlier, they'd had a perpetually mischievous expression. Now, they were more serious. His sandy hair was shorter. His fringe had been replaced by a longer version of a crew cut. I could pick out echoes of the Xander I had known but didn't fool myself that he was the same person.

"Oh, by the way, Dixie asked me to give you her contact details, in case you have any problems during your recuperation at home."

I did my best to hide my satisfaction, and he continued

"Here's my number too. In case you just need to talk, or have a beer. I know it can be boring, living alone. Anyhow, we're here"

With a quiet hum, the side door of the van slid open.

I felt in my jacket pocket and realised that, foolishly, I had no idea where my keycard was. My own clothes had been pretty much ruined in the attack, and Vanguard had provided replacements.

Alexander held out a sliver of shiny plastic.

"Lost something? We've been keeping an eye on the place for you. Hope you don't mind but we took the liberty of restocking your fridge, with a bit of advice from your D.D.A. as to what normally makes the shopping list."

I thought it a little over the top that Vanguard had gone to the trouble of querying my Domestic Assistant device to arrange a full larder for my return, but I wasn't going to complain.

"Cheers, Xander. Let's not leave it too long this time, eh?"

We shook hands and he got into the front passenger side of the van.

8

Chapter 8

I climbed the stairs to the second floor. Since waking from my long sleep, I seemed to have much more energy than before. Presenting my keycard to the scanner, the door opened with a click and I was home.

"Good morning, Jack. You're home early today. Is everything alright?"

"Fine thanks, Alice. Could you make some coffee, please."

"Of course."

The coffee grinder in the kitchen whirred into life as the apartment's Digital Domestic Assistant responded to my request.

On a table by the door were a couple of advertising leaflets, obviously picked up by whichever Vanguard operative had last been in the flat. Thankfully, since pressure from ecological lobbyists had made the excessive use of paper and wood products almost as unpopular as the now demonised plastics, the amount of junk mail in circulation had slowed to a trickle.

The same, unfortunately, couldn't be said for electronic soliciting, but I'd managed to clear most of the junk backlog remotely while in the Vanguard facility.

The only thing I'd not been able to clear down was the buffer on the electronic door controller. Its remote connectivity had been a little flaky before my enforced absence, so I'd need to check it locally.

"Alice, show me new EDC entries."

"Certainly, Jack. Do you want me to display on screen, or stream to your vGlasses?"

"Glasses, please, Alice."

I made one lense of my vGlasses opaque so I could review the footage, while leaving the other clear so I could navigate my way around the apartment and collect my coffee.

There wasn't much to see. The obligatory visit from one or other religious evangelist. You'd expect that in a resurrected city. The window cleaner had called twice and someone had attempted to leave a parcel for one of the other residents of the building.

I'd only had one caller I couldn't identify. An elderly man, with thinning grey hair and a Van Dyk beard which covered the lower part of a face which looked as if it had been badly scarred by acne many years previously. He dabbed at red-rimmed eyes with a white handkerchief and stared directly at the camera as if, in some way, he hoped to see someone on the other side of the lense. He didn't speak, ignoring Alice's enquiry, but turned, with a resigned look in his eyes and walked away. There was something familiar in his expression, but I couldn't put my finger on it.

Alice confirmed that he'd visited during the time I was unconscious in Vanguard's care.

Probably some preacher, wanting to show me the way to God. If only he knew how close I'd been at the time.

True to Xander's word, the larder was well-stocked but I wasn't much in the mood for eating and decided that, after three weeks of confinement, I needed some fresh air.

I changed into a t-shirt and shorts, throwing the Vanguard sweatsuit in the laundry, grabbed my vGlasses and headed for the great outdoors.

The streets of Crater City were wide and lined with young trees. Broad pavements kept the pedestrians away from the humming tide of electric traffic.

The sun was warm and bright. A little too bright, after my underground vacation. I took out my vGlasses and set them to a gradient tint.

As I strolled down towards the Hub, I examined my surroundings. It seemed to me that, even through my shades, the colours of the flowers and the grass were extraordinarily vibrant. Perhaps it was my brain's reaction to a period of virtual sensory deprivation. I'd spent more than two weeks in a coma, followed by days and nights cocooned in the subdued colours and lighting of the Vanguard facility.

That might also explain an apparent improvement in the acuity of my hearing. I could hear the buzz of the Taxees passing by, seemingly louder than I remembered. Conversations, not meant to be overheard by passers-by, assailed my ears. Even the birds and insects seemed determined to compete for my attention. Unfortunately, I had no equivalent of the vGlasses for my ears.

In addition to their intense colours, the flowers had also increased their scent output. Strolling between the planters was like walking past the testing bar in a perfume shop. I could even smell the moss, growing between the tree roots, damp and earthy.

I closed my eyes and inhaled the kaleidoscope of smells. I

opened them again in shock.

I closed them again, to make sure I wasn't imagining things.

I could still see. With my eyes closed. The image was distorted slightly and the colours bizarrely altered. It looked like a photograph in which different hues had been swapped. Blues had changed places with yellows, and greens with shades of orange.

I thought at first it was some sort of crazy after-image. The sort of thing you see, after staring at a bright light, then closing your eyes.

But this was different. When I turned my head, my point of view changed too. Instinctively, I inhaled through my nose. Suddenly the image sharpened, the colours intensified.

There was more. In this mind's eye vision, I could see the people around me. They glowed different colours and each left a trail in the air, behind them. I inhaled again and realised that I could smell each person. They all had individual combinations of scents and odours, and these hung in the air after they passed. I was seeing peoples' scent trails, like vapour trails behind a jet.

I panicked and opened my eyes again.

I looked around, checking to see if anyone had noticed my strange behaviour. They were all too wrapped up in their own realities to notice the struggle I was having with mine.

What was going on? Could it be some sort of brain damage, caused by the attack, the time my brain was without oxygen? Was it a side-effect of coma recovery?

I wondered if I should phone Doctor Dixon, then smiled. I was going to save that call for some time in the near future.

Trying to convince myself that this new talent was not the result of some sinister abnormality, I resumed my walk. The temptation to keep my eyes closed all the way down to the hub was almost irresistible, but I managed to overcome it and navigated my surroundings the old-fashioned way.

As I approached the small recreational area at the next junction, I could see Daisy by the entrance gate. I was never sure if he was homeless, but he was certainly harmless. He claimed to be one of the survivors of the Event. He would recount, to anyone who would listen, how he was on his way home to his wife and child when a giant rock from space exploded and obliterated the city and the life he knew.

Now he sat by the gate, in his faded parka, watching other people's families and children at play, smiling sadly to himself.

This time, however, he was not smiling. He was surrounded by a group of youths, who had decided to entertain themselves by tormenting him.

He carried his few belongings and mementoes in a Rainbow Unicorn rucksack. It was a gift he bought for his five-year-old daughter on the day his world ended. The largest of the gang, a red-headed youth, wearing a t-shirt with the word 'Dill' spray painted on the front, was shaking it. He spilled the contents out on to the ground and stamped on them. His companions laughed and jeered.

Normally, I would just feel annoyance and disappointment at such a display. Today, however, it seemed that it was not only my senses that were enhanced. My temper was more reactive too. I felt a wave of anger rising inside and strode over. I positioned myself between Daisy and the grinning youth.

"What the hell are you doing?"

"As if it's any of your business. Do one."

"Leave him alone." I said quietly, almost under my breath.

I had the urge to punch him. I fought to retain my composure.

"Or?" Hands on hips, smiling at his companions.

I leaned in close and snarled.

"Go. Now."

He stank of sweat and cheap body spray. As he spoke, I could smell cider on his breath.

"Seriously, Dude. Is showing me your teeth supposed to scare me?"

That was all I was going to take. Without another word, I grabbed the front of his shirt with both hands and lifted him off the ground.

He flapped his arms and legs like a pinned insect before I threw him over the fence and into a flower bed.

I turned and looked at the other lads in turn, as he had done, but I wasn't laughing.

They took the hint and ran.

Entering the playground, I found Daisy's tormentor, winded, on the floor. He tried to scrabble away on all fours as I stood over him.

"OK, Man. OK."

"Leave and don't ever bother him again."

He regained his feet and ran for the exit, pausing on the threshold to look back,

"Not done, Man. Wait and see." He made an obscene gesture and ran off after his companions.

I resisted the impulse to chase him and offer more discouragement.

My heart was pounding. What the hell did I just do? At least two of the lads were almost my equal in size and the one I had tossed was probably a couple of inches taller.

I returned to where Daisy was picking up his belongings.

I'd never seen him standing up before. He must have been over

53

six feet tall. Long blonde hair fell to his shoulders, matching his stubble. He looked like a Viking. If he'd been so inclined, he could have easily dealt with his tormentor himself. I guess he was just a pacifist.

"OK?"

He nodded, the bobble on his woolly hat bouncing back and forth.

"Thanks, but there was no need. They would've got tired soon enough"

"Sorry, I couldn't stand by and watch it happen."

"Hm. Good throw though."

His grin showed the gaps where he had lost a couple of teeth, but he was genuinely amused.

"Ah, yeah. Adrenaline, huh?"

Reassured that he was unhurt, I excused myself and went on my way, my hands shaking. I couldn't say whether it was with nerves, or exhilaration.

I stopped for a coffee at the centre of the Memorial.

It was formed of concentric circular walls breached at the cardinal points by pathways through to the centre.

The walls had been built of stone and brick recovered from the devastated city and were multi-coloured patchworks, bearing the names of as many of the dead as were actually known.

I watched the people coming and going, meeting and greeting and reflected on how close I had come to joining those named.

When I arrived back at the apartment, it was gone 4 pm and my stomach was beginning to remind me that I had missed lunch.

Rummaging through the provisions supplied by Vanguard, I found a tasty looking piece of steak. Fried up with a few shallots and accompanied by some oven roast mediterranean vegetables, it soon took the edge off my appetite.

After my recent confinement and enforced abstinence, a drink in the local seemed like an attractive idea, so I hit the bathroom.

The smart-loo flagged up on its display that I had lost six pounds since it last weighed me. I declined its request to provide a stool sample for analysis and slipped into a hot bubble bath.

A chime from Alice indicated an incoming call.

"Reply, voice only, please Alice."

"Hi, Jack?"

"Xander? Checking up on me?"

"Well, the job I was on has been cancelled so I've got the night off and wondered if you fancied going out for a drink."

"That's a coincidence. I'm getting ready to go out for one. Just in the bath at the moment, but can be ready in about thirty minutes"

"Thank God you didn't enable video. See you in half an hour."

"Meet you down at the Star?"

"I'll get them in."

As I was on enforced leave and had no acting work pending, I figured I might as well shave off the thick beard I had cultivated in Vanguard's care.

After cutting the excess with scissors, I lathered up and began to shave. With no mirror by the bath, I worked by touch.

As usual, I took extra care around the area of my scars, so as not to nick the raised flesh.

Only, this time, as I ran my fingers across my jaw, I couldn't feel them.

Disbelieving, I scrambled out of the bath, soaking the floor and wiped the steam off the mirror on the front of the bathroom cabinet.

Impossible. The scars were gone. I recalled Doctor Dixon saying the Vanguard surgeons were good, but she never mentioned they'd worked on my face.

My first thought was the possibility of rebooting my acting career. My second was to get down to the Star and quiz Xander.

9

Chapter 9

Throwing on some clean clothes, I almost ran out of the block and down the street in the direction of the local pub.

Realising I was going to arrive early, I slowed to a stroll.

I was so wrapped up in my own excited thoughts that I never noticed I had acquired an escort.

"Yo, Hero."

I recognised the scent immediately.

Just what I needed, the leader of the gang who had been hassling Daisy. And he'd brought more friends.

I kept walking

"Don't ignore me, bastard."

I began to extend my stride.

I was within running distance of the Star, and could probably have raced to safety, but I wasn't going to give him that satisfaction.

Suddenly, several pairs of hands grabbed me from behind and arrested my progress.

The tall youth stepped in front of me and smirked.

"Not showing your teeth this time, big man? Don't worry, you'll soon be picking them up off the pavement."

He pulled back his right arm and swung at me.

I pulled my arms together in front of me, shrugging off my captors like slipping off a coat.

For big lads, they didn't seem to be putting up much resistance.

I dodged sideways and my attacker's swing went wild. He lost his balance, stepping across in front of me.

I planted my foot firmly on his backside and pushed, sending him sprawling, full length, on the floor.

I was feeling quite pleased with myself.

Enraged, he jumped to his feet, shouting to his crew. "Get him. Hold him."

Any hope I had that the humiliation of being thrown to the floor might put him off quickly faded.

They recovered and jumped me again, shouting encouragement to the tall youth.

"Cmon, Dylan. Do the bastard"

I tried to shake them off, but they were better prepared this time and kept their grip.

There was a flash in the darkness, a reflection of the almost-full moon.

The one the others called Dylan crouched in front of me, tossing a knife from hand to hand.

I began to feel real fear.

He moved forward quickly and lunged.

Unable to free myself from the grip of the gang, I dropped to one knee and twisted my body, lowering my right shoulder.

It was enough to throw them off balance, and one of them slid over my body into the path of the oncoming blade.

A splash of blood hit me in the face and ran down into my mouth.

It galvanised me into action.

Grabbing the wrist of one of the other youths restraining me, I pulled and twisted as hard as I could.

Exerting more force than I expected, I was rewarded with a sickening crack. He screamed and released me. Holding his injured arm, he backed off.

The others were obviously discouraged and relaxed their hold. I pulled free.

They retreated, forming a loose semi-circle behind me.

Dylan crouched in front of me, knife in hand.

He waved it in front of him, like a matador teasing a bull.

I stood still. I was no street fighter, but knew enough to make him come to me. I reached into my pocket and brought out my phone, concealing it in my hand.

He stepped from side to side, swinging the blade in an arc.

I began to get the impression that he wasn't sure what to do next. His big scare tactic hadn't worked and now one of his gang was lying on the floor, bleeding and whimpering. Another was out of the fight, with a broken arm.

The lads behind me were getting restless.

"C'mon, Dill. Do 'im."

Emboldened by the pressure from his peers, Dylan surged forward, waving the knife in front of him.

Lifting my hand to the level of my face, I twisted my wrist quickly, to activate the instant torch function on my phone.

Blinded by the mini LED spot, Dylan began stabbing wildly.

I had already stepped to one side. With all the force I could muster, I kicked him hard in the crotch.

He grunted and doubled over, dropping the knife. I kicked it away, into the darkness.

Enraged by my tactic, the semicircle of youths closed behind me and tried to wrestle me to the floor.

I tensed myself to throw them off again, when a heavy weight landed on my back.

It was Dylan.

Gripping his right wrist with his left hand, he pulled his forearm tight across my throat, trying to strangle me. I knew that, if I lost consciousness, I was likely to suffer a severe beating but a red mist was coming down across my vision and my throat was burning. His right arm was across my cheek and I opened my mouth as wide as I could and sank my teeth into his flesh.

He squealed and loosened his grip. He tried to pull his arm away, but I wasn't letting go.

I bit down harder, feeling the skin part and his blood oozing into my mouth. It was hot and sweet.

He screamed louder, calling for the other gang members to help him but they released my arms and backed off, horrified.

I could hear someone running towards me. At the same time, Dylan's cronies were running away. He was writhing and twisting, squealing for me to release him. My jaws locked in anger. He wasn't getting away this time.

There was another voice.

"Jack...Nube... it's Xander. Let go."

I bit down harder still, Dylan's scream rising in pitch to a shriek.

Then I swallowed.

I'd been in the Police Station before but always through the back door, holo-cam in hand.

Sitting in the waiting room was a new experience.

The smell was atrocious, a mixture of urine, alcohol and fruit-flavoured inhalants overlayed with hints of vomit and body odour.

The walls were tiled for easy cleaning, which was long overdue.

Plastic benches lined the walls, covered in graffiti. Marker pen, burning or gouging seemed to be the favoured methods of leaving a lasting impression.

The caged CCTV obviously did little to discourage the practice.

The desk staff observed the area through a glass screen, protected by wire mesh.

Three doors led out of the room. To the exit, the unisex toilets and the passage through into the Station. I noticed that door had no handle on the outside.

As we waited, Xander tried to engage me in small talk. I wasn't in the mood. I couldn't believe what I'd just done. Sure, I'd been angry. I'd been afraid too, but adrenaline is no excuse for cannibalism.

My logical brain was engaged in a battle with something else inside my head. I knew my actions were reprehensible, but it seemed I was unable to feel guilt.

In fact, apart from the satisfaction of having won the fight, I actually felt annoyed with Xander for having intervened.

Dylan had been hauled away, kicking and squealing. A police escort had taken him for medical treatment. A separate vehicle had collected the youth with the broken arm, and the stabbing victim.

After about a half hour, the door swung open and Sergeant Morrison waved me through.

Xander followed.

"Hello, Jack. I saw the name on the interview sheet, but never expected it to be you."

"I wasn't expecting it myself, Sarge."

"Never had you pegged for a one-man army."

He led us into an interview room.

"Who's your friend?"

Xander passed his Vanguard ID to the Sergeant. He tilted it back and forth, looking at the holophoto.

He raised his eyebrows. "That's a new one."

"I'm just here as a witness, and a friend." offered Xander. "We were supposed to be meeting up at the Star for a couple of pints and, when I turned up, six or seven lads were having a go at Jack. I'm fairly sure one of them had a knife."

"Did you see the start of the fight?" Morrison asked.

"No. In fact, it was pretty much over by the time I got there. One of them had a chest wound, one had a broken wrist and Jack was trying to discourage one from strangling him."

"Discourage. Hmm. You do know, Jack, that removing chunks of muscle from one of these thugs, with your teeth, could be construed as bodily harm?"

"That's ridiculous." exploded Xander "They were trying to kill him."

"Calm down, Sir. As I said. COULD be. In this case, no charges will be filed. We've been after these lads for quite a while. They've been responsible for a number of assaults and robberies, and we have positive IDs so I think they'll be going down for quite a stretch. Once they're released from hospital that is.

Any idea why they targeted you, Jack?"

I told him about the incident with Daisy, earlier in the day.

He shook his head.

"Poor sod. Never did any harm to anyone. You've done us a favour, Jack. Just do us another one, though, eh? Try not to make holes in any more villains?"

I sheepishly agreed.

"Right," he concluded " just need a quick signature here, and you can get off. Got a pen on you? Some bugger's nicked mine"

"And in a Police Station too." teased Xander. "Here. Borrow mine."

A few short minutes later, we stepped out of the foul-smelling waiting room, into the cool night. I took a deep breath of fresh air.

We were virtually next door to the nearest pub and I now seriously needed a pint.

It wasn't the Star, but it served beer, and that was all I was interested in.

I grabbed a handful of salted nuts from the bar, while Xander ordered the drinks, wanting to taste something other than Dylan's blood in my mouth.

Given that the whole city had been rebuilt less than ten years ago, the pub had not aged well.

Strips of wallpaper were missing by the slot machines, where disgruntled gamblers had taken out their displeasure on the decor. The carpets didn't appear to have been cleaned since the place opened.

It was hard to find a bench seat where the upholstery wasn't cut, torn or just threadbare.

The same gougers who had left their mark on the thermoplastic benches in the Police Station had left similar inscriptions in the wooden surface of the table.

Xander held his watch up to the PayPanel, waited for the beep confirming his transaction, and returned from the bar with two pints.

"Here you go."

He scrutinised my face, with one eyebrow raised.

"Quite a defence you've got going on there. I don't remember learning that one in karate. Apparently, your post-Event therapy never included anger management."

I mumbled into my beer, swallowing a cool mouthful to calm a burning itch in my throat. I didn't appreciate his humour.

"You OK, Nube? You're looking very flushed."

I coughed, spitting beer all over the table.

Xander stepped back, arms wide, looking at the beer dripping down his shirt.

"Aw, come on!"

I tried to speak, but my throat was on fire. I couldn't swallow for a lump that seemed to be growing there.

"Nube? Speak to me."

One hand clutching at my throat, the other reaching out towards Xander, I struggled to breathe.

A rasping wheeze was all I could manage.

"Somebody call an ambulance."

Fighting to draw air into my lungs, I fell to the floor.

I felt as if Dylan were trying to choke me again.

I was sweating profusely, and I could hear my pulse pounding in my ears.

The landlord was standing over me, shaking his head.

"Nuts. It's the bloody nuts."

He grabbed my wrist.

The last thing I felt as a black veil came down over my eyes was a needle prick in my arm.

10

Chapter 10

As I came round, the first face I saw was that of Doctor Dixon. She was scrutinising me with an expression of concern.

"Doctor Dixon? What are you doing here?"

"I work here, Jack. Welcome back to Vanguard. You know, if you were so desperate to see me again, you could have just phoned."

I managed a weak smile.

"Believe me. I was planning on doing just that."

Looking around the cubicle, I could see that it was not the one I had previously occupied, but I obviously was not in the Accident and Emergency Department of Hope City hospital.

This room was windowless, even the heavy steel door leading out into the corridor.

The furniture was limited to my bed and a wheeled trolley at its side.

It looked more like a cell than a ward.

I tried to push down with my hands, to move myself back up the bed. Something was restricting my movements. I looked down to find that my wrists were immobilised by buckled leather straps.

I was wearing a hospital gown and there was an infusion running into my left forearm.

Something was not right. "What the hell?"

"Please, Jack. Stay calm. I'll explain everything in due course. You were thrashing and convulsing when you came in. We had to protect you and the Medical Staff."

"Well, I'm OK now, so you can take them off."

"I'm afraid that won't be possible just at the moment." She looked embarrassed.

"Then at least tell me what the hell I'm doing here."

"You appear to have suffered an extreme allergic reaction. What we refer to as anaphylaxis."

"You mean the nuts? But I'm not allergic to nuts."

"I know that, but the landlord suspected that you were. If he hadn't treated you with a micro adrenaline injector he keeps for his own allergies, you might not be with us now. Look at your right hand." She pointed.

The thumb and first two fingers were red and swollen, the skin almost blistered.

I thought back to the moment I entered the bar with Xander.

"That's wrong. I picked up the nuts with my left hand."

"Exactly. We need to determine what else you touched which may have triggered the reaction."

I struggled to remember.

"Well, the pub door, the police station door, the desk, my statement, a coffee cup. I don't know."

"You signed the statement?"

"Sure. Xander lent me a pen."

She raised an eyebrow.

"I'll be back in a second."

"What about these straps?"

The door closed behind her. I did not get a reply.

When she returned, Xander was with her.

"Am I glad to see you. Can you get her to take these straps off?"

"Not my call, Buddy. I'm afraid they'll stay on a little longer, given your recent violent behaviour."

"That was self-defence. " I was getting more frustrated.

"And earlier, when you threw him over the fence?"

"How do you know about that?"

His silence spoke volumes

"You've been watching me?"

"For your own good. Doctor Dixon thought there was a faint chance that your condition might... develop."

"Condition?"

"There's no easy way to put this, Jack. You may be infected." explained the Doctor.

I turned to face her.

"Infected. You mean...the attack?"

"Exactly."

"So what is it? Rabies? What?Can you treat me?"

Her face was a mask of concern.

"At this stage, we can't definitely identify the pathogen, nor predict how it will advance, let alone how to treat it."

I feared the worst."How long have I got?"

Her expression brightened.

"No, no. One thing we are relatively certain of is that the infection is non-fatal."

As I tried to assimilate the information, she turned to Xander.

"Agent Walters, do you have your pen?"

Xander produced it from his inside pocket and handed it to

her, puzzled.

"Jack. Could you hold this in your left hand, please."

I took the pen, reluctantly.

"Well, apart from the fact that I've never heard of anyone being allergic to a biro, if this does turn out to be the cause, won't I have the reaction again?"

"Don't worry, Jack. The infusion is an anti-allergenic. It should prevent any extreme reaction, such as anaphylaxis"

Should. Great.

"How do you know I'm not just allergic to swallowing scum-bag blood?"

"Well, I did consider that but, given the time elapsed from ingestion of blood and tissue to the time of your collapse, I think it unlikely. That wouldn't explain the pattern of marks on your hand, anyway. However, within the next month, I would recommend you are screened to ensure you haven't contracted any blood-borne diseases, such as hepatitis."

She smiled uncomfortably and tried to change the subject

"This is the first time I've seen you clean-shaven, Jack. I have to say it's an improvement."

She reached out and touched my cheek with the back of her hand. Her fingers were cool. I caught her eye, and tried not to smile. She withdrew her hand suddenly. A blush was barely visible in her cheeks. She risked a sideways glance, to see if Xander had noticed.

He was oblivious, but I thought it best to keep the conversation going, to avoid an awkward silence.

"That reminds me. I was meaning to ask you about the repair job your surgeons did on my face. That was some plastic surgery. Should help my career no end, if I ever get out of here"

She frowned and shook her head, then leant forward to

68

examine my chin.

"We never touched your face. You had a full beard when you came in."

My left hand was beginning to itch. I dropped the pen. It clattered on the bare floor.

"Steady, Nube. That was a present from my Gran."

I turned the hand over to reveal a developing red weal across the palm. The itch became a burning sensation.

"What the hell, Xander? Some sort of poison spy pen?"

"No, I swear. It was a present from my Grandmother on my twenty-fifth birthday. It's silver."

My brain leapt to a ridiculous conclusion.

"I'm allergic to silver? Are you trying to tell me I'm a vampire or something."

The Doctor looked me straight in the face, her expression serious.

"No, Jack. I'm sorry. In point of fact, I believe you may be turning into a werewolf."

I began to laugh

"You're crazy. This is all totally bloody insane. What is it, some sort of bad joke? Well, I'm not laughing. Let me out of here, now. Xander, help me."

He looked away.

I was beginning to get angry.

I started thrashing around, yanking at the restraints, which cut into my wrists, despite the padding.

The Doctor moved to the table beside the bed and picked up a syringe.

"Jack. Please stop. You'll injure yourself."

"Let me out. Take them off." I was shaking the bed.

"I'm sorry, Jack." She looked sincere. "You need to rest."

69

Inserting the needle in a port on the IV tube, she introduced a white fluid into the infusion.

My struggles became weaker and blackness swallowed me again.

11

Chapter 11

The Wolf was in my dreams. Only, this time, I knew what it was. I knew what I was, and I wasn't afraid.

The Wolf was in my dreams, and Death followed in his wake.

For the first time, I saw him in his entirety. He was old, silver, but huge and powerful. Standing on my four paws, my head barely reached his shoulder. He was the Alpha. I would follow where he led.

We weren't at the house, where we first met.

We walked the night, through unfamiliar streets, under the harsh illumination of LED streetlights.

Shunned by the local dogs, we walked alone, alert for the scent of Man. We weren't afraid but didn't invite discovery.

We loped through the sleeping city, ignoring the houses and the occasional lit windows, until we found the one we sought.

The painted wooden door collapsed in splinters before the onslaught of steely claws, driven by inhuman force.

As we stood in the hallway, sniffing the air, an elderly bearded man appeared at the top of the stairs.

His pale face was a picture of shock and fear as he turned and ran along the landing seeking to escape.

But there was no refuge from the roaring death which vaulted the stairs in a single bound and pinned him to the floor.

The Wolf dispatched him with a single slash to the throat.

There was no hope of resistance, no time to call for help.

There was no mercy.

The attack was not frenzied, as I had expected, but calm and methodical.

Emotionless, I watched as a human body was un-made and reduced to its component parts, blood, flesh, viscera and bone...

Afterwards, we sat amid the carnage. I could hear the voice of the Wolf, in my mind.

"You too have tasted the flesh of man." It was not a question.

"It was an accident." I was ashamed.

"I think not."

"What do I do, now?"

"We must find each other. I will teach you. You have much to learn and my time will soon be over. If they catch me, before my work is done, you must fulfil my legacy."

"I don't understand." Teach me? Teach me what? How to be a killing machine?"

The yellow eyes closed

"I am weary. I must go."

"No, wait. Tell me more. Why are you doing this?"

But he was gone, and there was only blackness.

12

Chapter 12

Blackness, broken by flashes of light.

I opened my eyes and looked around, struggling to focus.

There appeared to be gouges in the ceiling.

Except it wasn't the ceiling, it was the wall, and I was lying on my side, on the floor.

I was alone. Where was the Doctor? Or Xander?

I was no longer restrained. Naked, yes. Restrained, no.

Behind me, the bed leant upside down against the opposite wall. The steel frame was bent. The mattress lay in a corner, torn to pieces. Its filling spilled out on to the floor.

The hospital gown I had been wearing was in tatters and the bedding was scattered around in shreds

I gathered up some strips of blanket, and wrapped them around me, while I continued my examination of the room.

The walls were marked with deep parallel furrows. They looked as if they had been made by large claws. The steel door had suffered extensive denting from impacts on the inside, and there were long scratches in the painted surface.

The ceiling light housing had been damaged and the bulb inside was flickering. It was the only functioning light in the room. A small metal cage by the door appeared to have been torn from the wall in the far corner and contained the mangled remains of a CCTV camera.

What the hell had happened in here? If the Wolf had found me, why wasn't I dead. No, that didn't make sense. If the Wolf had been here, how had it escaped?

I checked the room for signs of blood. Had the Doctor and Xander been in the room during the destruction?

I shouted, and banged on the door, but could hear no reply from the other side. I didn't know if there was even anyone out there.

Finally, frustrated, I sat down on the remains of the ruined mattress and waited. I was cold and confused.

I must have dozed off, because I was woken by Xander lightly shaking my shoulder.

"Nube, are you good, Buddy?"

"Hm?"

"Looks like you had a wild night. Come on. Let's get you cleaned up."

Covering myself with the rags, I meekly followed him out through the battered steel door.

I was relieved to see another face. At least I wasn't alone. I had so many questions, but didn't know where to begin.

I felt as if I was no longer in control of my own life. I let him lead me down the corridor and into a side room.

Clean clothes were piled on a bed, and a shower was running in the en-suite.

I closed the bathroom door behind me and dropped the remains of the blanket on the floor.

Like someone still in a dream, I negotiated the shower curtain, and turned my face to the water.

When I emerged from the shower, and dressed, a cooked breakfast awaited me on the bedside table. I hadn't realised, but I was ravenous and ate, almost without chewing.

By the time Xander reappeared, I was beginning to feel a little more human. He brought a tray carrying three cups of coffee, and Doctor Dixon followed him in.

She looked tired and strands of her normally immaculate hair had fallen across her face.

She smiled. There was no joy in her expression. She looked embarrassed, ashamed, even.

"Jack. I'm so sorry about yesterday. I had no idea what might happen and had to take precautions. I had you sedated most of the day. I realise we may have caused you some distress, but we had to consider everyone's safety."

Accepting that I probably already knew the answer, I asked "What happened in that room?"

"You did, Buddy."

Xander's face was grim

"Me?"

"Well, you went in and you came out so, if you can think of another name for what was in there . ."

He left the sentence unfinished, but Doctor Dixon continued.

"We have video footage, up until the camera was destroyed. I warn you, it may be difficult to watch, but it might help you accept the reality of your situation."

"Situation? What a wonderful euphemism."

She looked away. Embarrassed or impatient, I couldn't tell.

I regretted hurting her feelings, but was still angry at her for anaesthetising me. That had been a breach of trust.

75

"OK, Doc. Let's see it."

She located the file on her phone and cast it to the screen on the wall, at the foot of the bed.

Watching a video of yourself, sedated and strapped to a cot, is not an experience I would recommend. Especially when it's accompanied by the uneasy feeling that things are about to take a turn for the worse.

She skipped along the timeline along until the motionless figure on the bed began to stir.

Initially, it looked as if I was having difficulty breathing, gulping in larger and larger breaths of air. My chest was expanding with each inhalation, but not shrinking as I exhaled. Soon my torso was like a barrel and totally out of proportion to my body.

I lifted my head from the pillow, looked around, then began to bang my head backwards with force on the bed. I winced, just watching it.

Although the sound was muted, it was obvious that I was shouting or screaming.

My mouth was wide open, as were my eyes, and my face was contorted, with rage or pain. I couldn't tell.

Fighting to release myself from the wrist straps, my shoulders lifted from the bed and the muscles in my upper arms began to swell as I increased my efforts. I could see the veins bulging, just below the skin.

My legs drummed rhythmically on the mattress. The bed began to shake and the blanket slid to the floor.

As I howled, my jaw appeared almost to dislocate. My facial features began to elongate, as if made of rubber. They morphed into the shape of a muzzle. From the sides of my mouth, white foam overflowed on to the pillow.

Transfixed, I watched as my skin appeared to change colour. Looking closer, I realised that it was actually sprouting thick brown hair.

My arms began to stretch, as if pulled by some unseen force, and hooked black claws burst through the skin at my fingers and toes.

My whole musculature swelled. It was like watching a time-lapse video of a bodybuilder's training progress.

When the creature's muzzle next opened, it was lined with glistening white fangs.

It was no longer human. I corrected myself. It was no longer me.

Suddenly the struggling stopped.

The beast looked down at the wrist straps and, with a single flex of its immense biceps, tore the restraints from their mountings.

With a fluid movement, more feline than canine, it rolled from the bed and landed on all fours.

Only then did I realise that it also had a tail.

It began to pace the room, its heavily muscled shoulders rippling with each step, sniffing at the bedding, the table and moving towards the door.

Its size made it hard to reconcile with the human being it had been only minutes before.

Approaching the door it reared up on its hind legs. It looked less like a wolf and more like some nightmare beast-human hybrid. It appeared to be just as comfortable on two legs as on four.

The claws raked at the door, trying to find a handle or opening mechanism.

Failing, it howled in frustration and began to pummel the metal with its front paws, which were curled into grotesque caricatures of human fists.

The door refused to yield. The enraged monstrosity unleashed its anger on the contents of the room, picking up the bed as if it were weightless and throwing it against the wall.

The talons demonstrated their destructive power as first the bedding, then the mattress and finally the walls fell prey to frenzied attack.

When nothing remained on which to vent its rage, the animal returned to its exploration of the room, sniffing each corner and scent marking.

Finally, it fixed its yellow eyes on the camera and the lense was misted by its moist breath as it came closer to investigate.

Before the mist could clear, a clawed hand struck at lightning speed and the picture was replaced by visual static.

They were both watching me, wondering how I would react.

I continued staring forward, mesmerised by the pattern of black and white dancing on the screen.

Proof positive of the existence of werewolves is hard enough to process. Having to accept that you are one of them has a tendency to overload one's brain.

I was stunned into silence.

My reverie was broken by the arrival of Agent Simons.

"Glad to see you're feeling yourself again, Mr Allman."

"Is that a joke?"

"Easy, Nube"

"And will you stop calling me that, for God's sake, Xander. Especially given the circumstances."

Simons looked puzzled.

"Circumstances?"

"It goes back to when Nube . . Jack and I were at school. We were studying the Egyptians, and their gods. There's one called Anubis, with the body of a man, and the head of a jackal. The teacher, unfortunately, described it as a jackalman and Jack Allman was henceforth known as Anubis. You know how pretentious Grammar School kids can be. Anyhow, it was shortened to Nube, and stuck. But, given that the jackal is a close relative of the wolf, I can see how it might be a sore point at the moment. Sorry, Jack"

"Whatever. So what happens now?"

Simons sighed.

"That rather depends on you, Mr Allman."

"Meaning?"

"You pose quite the dilemma. We have no grounds to hold you but you must accept, based on the video you have just watched, that you could present a significant risk to the Public if we release you."

"So, what? I'm a prisoner."

"Let's call it quarantine, until we have a clearer view of the situation."

Whatever he wanted to call it, it sounded as if I had little choice but to comply.

Forty-eight hours earlier, Fate had tempted me with the tantalising promise of a chance to kickstart my acting career.

That had now been snatched away and replaced with a situation which threatened my very liberty.

As I pondered the prospect of another bout of Vanguard hospitality, a nagging memory needled my brain. I pondered the half-formed suspicion until, finally, I raised the question.

"Was there another killing last night?"

Simons gave Xander a sideways glance.

"Now why would you ask that?"

"Yes, or no?"

"There was an incident, very similar to the one where we first met, yes."

"The victim was an older man, with a beard."

Simons did not look altogether convinced.

I continued.

"He was killed on the landing, at the top of a curved staircase."

Now I had his attention

"But, how?"

"I don't know. It's as if I had some kind of connection with the killer. I could see what was happening."

"I don't suppose you saw his face?"

"Not 'his', 'its'. The Wolf did this."

I paused, the seed of an idea continued to grow in my brain.

"How many more have there been?"

Simons looked at his feet and exhaled slowly

"With last night, that makes seven. Starting in Eastern Europe last year, then spreading across Central Europe to arrive in the UK a couple of months ago."

"The night I was brought back to Vanguard was a full moon. Were they all?"

He nodded.

"The theory had been floated before, and dismissed. The assumption was that the dates, perhaps, held some ritual significance. After seeing your metamorphosis last night I now think differently."

Xander interjected

"That makes our job even more difficult. How do you catch a killer who changes into an animal to commit a crime? And once you catch him, how do you convict him?"

His colleague smiled grimly.

"I wasn't planning on taking him alive."

"Might 'present a significant risk' if you did?"

"Don't worry Mr Allman. I regard you as an asset in this investigation, not one of its targets."

"So let me help. Take me to the scene of the crime. I may be able to pick something up that your tech toys miss, or it may jog my memory and provide some clue."

I desperately needed to regain some control. My current status of victim and bystander made me feel vulnerable and helpless.

Thankfully, Simons accepted my proposal.

"Agreed, on the proviso that we are back here before nightfall. There's nothing to suggest that the transformation occurs on any night other than the full moon, but I'd rather not take any chances."

He set off down the corridor. With a last glance at the Doctor's anxious face, I followed.

13

Chapter 13

Simons drove us to the scene.

Thanks to the hub and spoke design of the streets, we quickly crossed one side of the residential ring, and passed through the city centre to our destination on the other side.

I could never have found the house on my own, but instantly recognised the facade as we pulled on to the street, the shattered door a foretaste of what I knew lay inside.

The police cars, with their pulsing blue strobes, were a flashback to the first time I met Simons. I had no fear of being attacked, this time.

His ID card granted us passage through the police cordon.

Stepping over the threshold, the smell of blood hit me like a wave, far more intense than I recalled from the previous crime scene. I stood at the bottom of the staircase, trying to reconcile the grisly reality with the dreamlike quality of the previous night's vision.

Overall-clad Vanguard agents were painstakingly examining the scene.

We picked our way up the stairs, careful not to disturb any of the once-human debris adhering to the carpet.

Simons began taking report from one of the field agents.

I stood over the scene of the kill and closed my eyes.

I could still see my surroundings. The pseudo-colours of my scent radar gave the scene a psychedelic aspect.

During my connection to the Beast, I had been able to smell the victim's sweat. I had smelled his fear, how he lost control of his bladder before the attack sundered his flesh. Then all other odours were overwhelmed by the scent of blood.

In reality, and after the passage of time, the scent landscape had changed subtly.

The primary scent was still of blood but the faint whiff of putrefaction was beginning to assert itself. And .. something else.

"Simons, you need to get everyone outside. Now."

Without questioning, he ushered the crime scene techs into the street and stood back, to see what I would do next.

To anyone with no knowledge of the preceding day's events at Vanguard, my actions would have appeared eccentric at best.

Positioned in the centre of the landing, I tipped my head back slightly, eyes closed, nostrils flared.

Turning my head from side to side, I attempted to isolate the source of the rogue scent.

I had it. Eyes still closed, but navigating the scent landscape like a bloodhound following a trail, I strode to the end of the passageway. I stopped and opened my eyes, to find myself in front of a heavy bookcase.

I closed my eyes again and listened intently.

"Simons, you hear that?"

"I don't hear anything."

"Trust me. Behind this bookcase. There's someone breathing. It's very slow and shallow, and their pulse is weak, but they're

83

alive."

I tried to pull it away from the wall, but couldn't get sufficient leverage. It must have been screwed in place.

Simons raised an eyebrow but, overcoming his disbelief, he called the techs back in and demanded a crowbar.

"Get this bookcase away from the wall, now."

He dismissed protests from the investigators over the possibility of destroying evidence.

"We already have one dead victim. I'm more interested in preserving a life than your samples. Now get on with "

The wood groaned and splintered as it was pried away from the wall.

Except it wasn't a wall.

The cabinet had been bolted to a heavy steel door.

On the outside were heavy cast hinges but there were no handles, and no indication of how we might gain entry.

I pressed my ear to the cold metal. I could hear more clearly now. The sighing, slow respiration. The rapid, feeble pulse.

I nodded to Simons. He was already on his phone.

"Walters, we're at the Alekovic house. Get hold of the plans and see if there's any reference to a panic room. We need remote unlock access immediately. Oh, and send our ambulance and have Doctor Dixon prepare a bay."

He turned to me.

"I don't know how you did that Mr Allman, but you may just turn out to be even more of an asset than I imagined"

Then he was back supervising the techs in their unsuccessful attempts to gain purchase on the seamless steel door with their crowbars.

His phone rang.

"You have? Good. Everyone, step away from the door."

From inside the door, we could hear the whine of a motor and the sliding of heavy bolts.

The sound stopped and, with a faint sigh, the door moved a fraction.

Stepping forward, Simons grabbed the edge and swung it fully open.

Inside the cramped space, prostrate on a mattress on the floor, lay an elderly woman in a nightdress.

Unconscious, barely breathing, but definitely alive.

Simons was first into the room. Sweeping her up as if she were weightless he carried her down the stairs, to await the Vanguard ambulance. Her eyes flickered open momentarily as the cool air from outside stirred the hair on her forehead. Looking Simons directly in the eye, she whispered a single word.

"Vukodlak."

14

Chapter 14

We were back at Vanguard before dark, as Simons promised.

Before that day, I'd had no idea where it was located, having come and gone in windowless vans. I was surprised to find that it was in the industrial ring.

From the outside, it was a squat two storey structure not unlike a steel mill. There was no signage to distinguish it from the surrounding buildings. There was a single front pedestrian entrance with a reception desk and a gated ramp leading to an underground car park.

Once inside, it was obvious that the majority of the building was below street level.

Simons explained that the building of the new city had been the ideal opportunity for Vanguard to move from its previous location, just outside the capital.

With so much construction taking place, no-one would notice lorries leaving day and night, laden with soil as the construction company hollowed out the ground beneath the unassuming shell above. There were at least ten subterranean levels.

We exited the lift on level seven and I was ushered back into the hastily repaired secure room.

"Shouldn't be long, old chap." Simons reassured me "Once the moon comes out, so long as the Wolf doesn't, we can release you."

I sat on the edge of the bed, like a condemned man awaiting a stay of execution, examining my hands and fingers, half imagining I could see the claws erupting through the skin. At least I wasn't restrained this time. The events of the previous night had proved how futile that would be.

After around half an hour, following a panic attack caused by a misinterpreted cramp in my left leg, the door opened and Simons entered, accompanied by the Doctor.

"Well, I don't know about you," he smiled cheerily "but I could definitely do with some dinner."

We took the lift up to the communal area and walked through to the canteen. Within half an hour, we were sitting down to a hot meal worthy of any restaurant.

Xander had joined us, and opened the conversation, "So it's just the one night then, Doc?"

Doctor Dixon paused between forkfuls "It appears so although, even in his normal form, Jack appears to have retained some of his lupine abilities, according to Agent Simons' account."

"Loopy what now?"

"Certain wolf-like characteristics appear to carry over into Jack's normal life. The acute senses of smell and hearing for a start and, you also witnessed an increase in physical strength prior to the transformation, didn't you, Alexander?"

"Yeah, along with a pretty short temper."

"I'm rather more interested in the less commonplace abilities." interrupted Simons, reaching for his water glass "Like the ability to get inside the head of a serial killer."

I shook my head "So in one day I go from being human to

87

werewolf, to psychic werewolf. That's something new to put on my C.V."

"I don't think you're going to need a C.V. for your next job, Mr Allman," Simons replied. "I'd like to ask you if you would be interested in joining us at Vanguard."

"Well, I..."

"I appreciate you think you already have a life and career although it's not hard to see how your current condition could upset both of those.

Bear in mind, also, that we are very well equipped to investigate your 'affliction' and help you to manage it, while you work for us.

We can also offer you a safe environment to which you can retreat on your, shall we say, 'off' days."

"It's an interesting offer, but.."

He waved a hand to stop me. "Before you make a decision, I must point out that, unfortunately, there is a flipside to that coin. Were you not securely contained on those particular days, you could then potentially become as big a threat as the one we already face, which would put you on our radar for an entirely different reason."

There was no mistaking his meaning. I didn't much care for the implied threat.

Unfortunately, I had to admit he was right. I couldn't just drop off the face of the earth, once a month, in either of my current careers.

I looked across at Xander. He was watching me, expectantly.

"Hobson's choice it is, then. Where do I sign up?"

"Excellent decision, Mr Allman. Welcome to the Team."

He inclined his head, and tilted his water glass, as if in a toast.

I returned the nod. "But I still get to go home?"

"Of course." scoffed Simons "We're not in the habit of providing our agents with free accommodation."

"So what makes Vanguard the experts on werewolves?"

"Apart from the fact we've been tracking one for months?" Xander chimed in, to be interrupted again by Simons.

"In truth, your condition is pertinent to our current investigation. Apart from the perpetrator sharing your abilities, all of the victims have been, in some way or other, connected to a research project in the former Soviet Republic of Yugoslavia. We believe that the focus of their work was on lycanthropy."

"So a werewolf is killing the werewolf researchers?"

"That's how it looks" assented Xander.

"So how does this help me?"

Doctor Dixon raised a hand "Perhaps I can answer that.

We have had little or no luck obtaining information from the Eastern European crime scenes, or any of the Agencies which might hold records on the Yugoslavian research project. However certain documents have been found at the Western European and UK crime scenes relating to the work they were carrying out in the late 90's.

While it's by no means a complete record of their findings, it should go along way towards helping us to understand your condition and, with luck, finding a way to manage it."

"Thanks, Doctor. That's almost reassuring."

Simons phone rang. "Yes. Good. Did she say anything? Thank you. That's excellent news."

He slipped the mobile back into his suit pocket "An unexpected development. Milena Alekovic, the woman you helped save, Mr Allman, regained consciousness.

She says she has important information for us. Including the name of our killer.

Hedoen Volkov"

Dressed, and with makeup applied, Milena Alekovic bore little resemblance to the near-lifeless body Simons had carried from the panic room.

Her silver hair was scraped back, exposing a determined expression on her strong-boned face.

Simons introduced us "Agents Walters and Allman"

I tried to ignore Xander's amused sideways glance, assuming that my sudden 'promotion' was the simplest way to explain my presence without revealing my true role in her rescue.

She wasted no time on niceties.

"You must kill this creature before more good people die."

"Creature?" queried Simons.

"Please do not think to play games with me. You know exactly what you are hunting. Vukodlak, skin-walker, shapeshifter. Call it what you will, but it has to be destroyed."

"And you say you know its, his, name?"

"Hedoen Volkov." she spat "My husband worked with him and his people, trying to find a cure for the curse which beset them. The research project ended. As did many, with the collapse of the Yugoslav republic. Dmitri and his colleagues, they had no choice but to wind up their research and leave. They tried to explain to the villagers, but they refused to accept it and attacked the laboratory, destroying it."

"Villagers?"

"Volkov was the 'hetman' of a tribal group which lived isolated from other local communities. Their 'condition' bred fear and resentment and they kept themselves apart. My husband's work was aimed at bringing an end to their troubles and helping them to reintegrate as productive members of society."

"Very magnanimous." muttered Xander, immediately trans-fixed by hard stares from Simons and Milena alike.

"Of course, there were other potential advantages to the research." she continued. " Disease was virtually unknown within the tribe. Their recuperative and healing powers were remarkable, as was the average lifespan of the community. Volkov must, by now, be somewhere around 160 years old. Imagine the possible advances in medical science"

"But what makes you so certain Volkov is the killer, and what are his motives?" asked Simons.

Milena shook her head, slowly.

"My husband still had links with some of his old colleagues, a loose association of like-minded academics.

After the first killing, we heard rumours that Volkov was investigating the whereabouts of the remaining scientists from the project. Some of his methods of obtaining information were, shall we say, indelicate and attracted attention.

As to his motives, I have no idea. Relatively few of Dmitiri's colleagues are still alive and now all in their seventies and eighties. If Volkov is seeking revenge for some imagined injustice, he has waited almost forty years to extract it."

"Would your husband have any data or notes relating to his work, which might help us in our enquiry?"

"There are notes, but I don't know how they will help you catch a murderer."

"It's about trying to identify his motivation and perhaps find a pattern to his killings. Would you be able to put us in touch with any surviving members of his team? If we know who his targets are, we may be able to get a step in front of him and even protect them. Agent Walters can help you compile a list, along with organising collection of your husband's research. We would like you to stay here, at least for the moment, for your own safety.

Thank you for help and, once again, I'm sorry for your loss." He turned to me.

"Agent Allman, do you know how to fire a gun?"

Trying to disguise the surprise on my face, I followed him out.

Unsurprisingly, my response to his question was 'no'. Unless, of course, you were to count the rayguns I had discharged in my former life as space pirate.

Thinking about it, my work experience was pretty limited.

Apart from spending some time on both sides of a camera, I had very little in the way of transferable skills, and was beginning to wonder how much of an 'asset' I might be to Simons, and Vanguard.

My life hadn't been perfect before the attack but I had, at least, a steady income. My lack of achievement was matched by a corresponding lack of concern for the immediate future.

And now?

'We believe you may be turning into a werewolf'

I began to consider the full meaning of Doctor Dixon's statement.

At the time, I had refused to accept it. It crossed my mind that it might be an elaborate hoax. Admitted, having your throat almost torn out by an angry beast is rather more brutal than the usual hidden-camera set-up but hearing the word 'werewolf' the shutters of reason slammed down. It had no place in the real, logical world. I was an actor. I knew the difference between reality and fantasy. I stepped between one and the other but now I was being told the boundaries had moved?

The ridiculous assertion had confused me, sure, but finding

myself restrained and then being pumped full of drugs had scared the hell out of me. Being held prisoner by agents of a semi-secret organisation was much more real than being told I was about to change into a B-movie bogeyman.

And then I'd seen the video recording.

By the time I'd finished watching it, any hope of it being a fake had faded. Why would they? What would be the point of wasting time and resources to convince me of something so ludicrous?

My mind numbly accepted the recording as fact.

What I had to process now were the consequences. My whole life had changed.

Questions began to snowball in my brain. Could I be cured? Would I end up a salivating killer like Volkov? What part would I play in his pursuit and what would Vanguard do with me, once he was caught? Could I go back to my normal life, spending one night a month in a reinforced cell? Would I keep up my day job, like a secret identity? Was I really going to live to be a hundred and sixty years old?

As my brain ground to a halt, overwhelmed by the changes it was trying to accommodate, my feet followed suit. I stopped dead in the middle of the corridor. Simons looked back over his shoulder.

"Is there a problem, Mr. Allman?"

"I need some answers, and I need them now."

His irritation was clear.

"As you wish. I suggest you start with Doctor Dixon, then come and see me tomorrow."

He strode off down the corridor, leaving me to try and find my way to the Doctor's office.

15

Chapter 15

Doctor Dixon was at her desk, examining the contents of yellowed cardboard archive boxes.

"How are you, Jack?"

"Well enough, for someone who's recently found out he's a supernatural monster. Werewolves. Seriously? How is it even possible?"

"Well, I think you can drop the 'supernatural' label. Everything that's happening to you can be explained scientifically. It's remarkable but in no way magic.

To put it in simple terms you undergo a metamorphosis, changing from one form to another. The process isn't unknown in the animal kingdom. Tadpoles become frogs and caterpillars become butterflies.

What is extraordinary, in the case of lycanthropy is not only the speed of the transformation but the fact that it's reversible."

"But what about all the full moon business. That's real?"

"The human body has an unconscious awareness of the passage of time. Hormones are released at different times of day, relating to our sleep/wake rhythms, and the female menstrual cycle is regulated on a monthly clock so it's not unfeasible that the transformation is triggered in the same way."

"So it's controlled by hormones?"

"The Yugoslavian experiments appear to have identified a hormone which may be responsible for the process. They called it Volsine. It's not clear from the notes where it is produced but there's a suggestion that initial infection with the pathogen triggers activity in a small organ, previously believed to be vestigial."

"Vestigial?" I was trying to keep up with her explanation, but it might as well have been black magic.

"Not believed to perform any function in modern anatomy, like the appendix. The Volsine-producing organ is only present in less than 0.1% of the current population. That makes you quite a rarity, Jack." She smiled.

"Sounds more like a throwback."

"Well, more of an evolutionary dead-end. The stories of lycanthrope actually go back to ancient Greece but, with evolution hindering inheritance of the organ, the total potential and actual population has been reducing over time. Volkov's tribe was a freak cluster where heredity favoured the lycanthropes."

"So, is there any hope of a cure?"

"Cure? No. Not yet, at least." She frowned as she delivered the bad news.

"With a complete sequencing of the lycanthrope genome and further research to identify which genes are responsible for development of the organ, therapies could be developed to prevent its growth but, once a receptive subject is infected, the organ triggers on a monthly cycle, flooding the body with Volsine each full moon."

"And there's no way to block it?"

The lines in her forehead deepened. She held up one of the

yellowed folders.

"That's the odd thing about the research project. Agent Simons told me that Mrs Alekovic said the scientists were working to control the condition. The notes seem to contradict that. The main thrust of their work was concerned with triggering the transformation, including early experiments on the manufacture of a synthetic form of Volsine which could initiate the change, outside of the monthly cycle."

"Hm. I was kind of looking for the 'off' button, rather than the 'on' switch."

"I'm sorry, Jack. I wish I had better news for you." She dropped the file on the desk and rested her hand on my forearm. "I'm expecting Alexander to bring me some more files shortly. There's no saying what they may hold. At any rate, I have a much deeper understanding of your condition than I had when the attacks first began. Don't lose hope."

She removed her hand, but I could still feel the warmth through my sleeve.

"Thanks for the update, Doctor. I'll leave you to work. I need to go home and do some thinking."

The next morning, I made my way back to the corridor where Simons and I had parted company, and asked a passing agent for directions.

Simons raised his head from the pile of paperwork, as I entered his office.

"More questions, Mr.Allman?"

"To be honest, I was wondering how I'm any help to you. I'm okay with the idea of being drafted as an Agent but I have no training and very little idea of what to do, in this situation. I just need to figure out what's going on and what happens next."

"I understand. Sit"

He pushed his paperwork aside and laced his fingers together, resting his chin on top.

"Vanguard, or at least this office, is involved in an on-going investigation of a series of murders. All of the victims have a connection to the lycanthrope research lab in the former Yugoslavia. All of the murders have followed the same pattern, the victims torn apart, apparently by an animal.

The initial theory was that it was a trained beast, possibly with a handler who facilitated its entry into the murder scenes. Vanguard, however, has a background in handling cases which fall outside the areas of expertise of regular law enforcement so we were quick to realise, and accept, that the perpetrator was himself a lycanthrope."

"Just like that, you believe in werewolves?" I wished I had found it so straightforward.

"I did say that we are not regular law enforcement. However, until the night of your attack, we had not had physical contact with the killer. We collected samples of his blood from the scene. You may remember me shooting him. That, along with your developing condition and, ultimately, the statement from Mrs Alekovic should satisfy even the most sceptical."

"And now you have a name."

"More than a name. We have a face. Volkov flew into the UK on his own passport.

At the time there was nothing to link him to the murders, so no flags were raised.

It's a shame the Alekovic's and their network of colleagues didn't communicate their suspicions earlier. We could have been waiting for him."

He handed me a slate, displaying a black and white photograph.

"I know him."

Volkov looked tired, but certainly nowhere near his 160-odd years. His receding white hair and matching neat beard gave the impression of a man in his seventies. His watery eyes looked out of his pock-marked face, exactly as I had first seen them on my Electronic Door Controller recording.

"He came to my apartment."

Disbelief from Simons "What? When?"

"While you were treating me, following the attack. He was recorded by my EDC."

"How the hell did he find you?" Simons was obviously concerned. "This may suggest he's not working alone. He must have some local intelligence."

He looked me directly in the face.

"I'll be honest, Jack. I'm not sure exactly what part you will play in this investigation but you are obviously of interest to Volkov. That and your psychic connection to him may be pivotal in helping us identify both his motive and his location.

Your background in the recording of crime scenes, along with your apparently enhanced senses also make you valuable in the examination of evidence. We have no idea what new abilities you may present next.

I'd like you to work closely with Doctor Dixon. If she can come up with some method to reverse the transformation, not only will it help you, but it may provide us with a method to stop Volkov. After all, it's a lot easier to take down a 160 yr old man, than a 300 lb wolf. Which reminds me, there's still the matter of firearms training."

"Seriously? I need to carry a gun? This is Hope City, U.K. not downtown New York."

It seemed to be my day for annoying Simons. Rising from his desk, he brushed past me, into the corridor. He indicated for me to follow, but continued talking to me, over his shoulder, as we walked briskly through the complex, to a section I had not seen before.

"Make no mistake, Mr Allman. We are not your local constabulary. Some of the subjects we deal with are classified as extremely dangerous. Faced with the type of creatures we encounter, in a life or death situation, you will be more than grateful to have a weapon with which to defend yourself. A moment, if you please."

Passing his I.D. card over a scanner, he opened a metal door and stepped inside.

We entered a brightly-lit room. In front of us was a counter, behind which the room was divided into lanes, marked by plexiglass partitions. This was a firing range.

An agent in a bullet-proof vest was shaking Simons' hand. Simons turned to make introductions.

"Jack Allman, meet Diego Mochales, our weapons instructor.

Mochales stood around five feet six, with dark curly hair and a complexion which betrayed his mediterranean heritage.

Dredging up my secondary school Spanish, I attempted "Buenos días, señor Mochales."

His grin was as broad as his australian accent. "Cheers, mate. I appreciate the effort, but you're a couple of generations too late."

Seeing the confusion on my face, he continued.

"Great Granpa left Spain in the 1930's, to escape the civil war and start afresh in the New World. That included ditching the lingo and going native. All that's left of the old country now is his name, which Dad decided to bless me with, and Great Granma's recipe for squid."

Despite his tendency for over-sharing, I instantly liked Diego.

"Well, pleased to meet you, anyway."

"Likewise." He held out his hand.

Simons was already in the doorway.

"Do what you can, Diego. Mr Allman has never handled a weapon before, but it would be very useful if you could bring him to some basic level of competence sooner, rather than later."

"Will do, Boss." Diego waved to Simons as he exited.

He grinned again. "Ignore the miserable old sod." he advised. "I know he stomps around as if he's got a brush handle up his arse, but he's a good boss. If he didn't have a fair opinion of you, you would never have made it down here."

I mulled over the revelation. It was hard to determine what Simons was thinking at any given moment. He certainly had his own agenda and did not seem overly inclined to share it.

Diego opened a cupboard under the counter and produced a gun, a pair of ear protectors and a pair of goggles.

His own ear defenders hung around his neck and his goggles were pushed up over the top of his hair.

He handed me the gun. It was cold, and heavier than I had expected. I wrapped my hand around the butt and put my finger over the trigger.

"Okay. Stop there." he cautioned. "Unless you're about to shoot, keep your finger outside the guard. That's why I'm wearing a vest. You'd be amazed how many rounds can end up flying about, just because a rookie puts a little too much pressure on the trigger at the wrong time. Especially if their weapon is set to auto. Thankfully, that's not a real gun, but it's important to learn the lessons now."

"Not a real gun?" I turned it over in my hand and examined it.

It looked real enough to me.

"It's a replica, with a few enhancements, to facilitate training. It'll recoil like a real gun, and it will be as loud, but it can't fire live rounds."

"So how do I learn to shoot?"

"AR my man, good old AR. Slip on your goggles."

I put the gun down and did as I was told. The goggles were heavier than regular glasses. Diego busied himself at a keypad and the world went black. A second later, my vision returned and Diego was looking at me.

"OK? I just initialised the Augmented Reality routines. Those are a heavy duty version of your vglasses, linked to the firing range network. Look down the range."

I positioned myself between two of the plexiglass screens and looked towards the far wall.

"Here we go." mumbled Diego then, louder "You see it?"

A circular target had appeared, apparently hanging in midair, halfway down the lane.

"Right. Headset on." he instructed, positioning his own. I noticed his had a small microphone beside his right cheek.

When he next spoke, I could hear him in my ear defenders.

"Pick up the gun. That's good. Keep your finger outside the guard. Now, use your other hand to steady it. It's quite a weight, until you get used to it."

I was holding the gun with both hands around the butt. He quickly corrected me.

"If you keep your left hand that high, when the slide comes back, it will take the skin off. Cup it under your other hand, safely out of the way. That's better. Point at the target. Exhale. Squeeze the trigger slowly."

Even with the ear defenders on, the noise was deafening in

the confined space. The gun kicked upwards, as if it were trying to escape my grip. I almost dropped it. I suddenly felt a great deal more respect for the weapon in my hand. This was no toy. I could as easily injure myself as anyone else, if I didn't handle it properly.

I looked over at Diego, the shock clear on my face.

He grinned broadly. "You have seriously never fired a hand-gun before?"

"Well, they have been illegal in the UK, since the end of the last century, so the opportunity never presented itself. I don't know what I expected, but that was more than a bit scary."

"Glad to hear it. I wouldn't want you getting overconfident at this stage. But let's take a look at the target."

The virtual target zoomed towards me, on the AR display of the vgoggles. It consisted of seven concentric circles. The inner three were black, and the outer rings white. In the first white ring, outside the black centre circles, was a red dot. Diego nodded his head. "Beginner's luck? Let's try again."

The red dot vanished, and target retreated towards the far wall.

On Diego's order, I raised the weapon again, aimed, exhaled, and pulled the trigger.

This time I was more prepared for both the recoil and the noise and controlled the gun better as it kicked back.

The shot wasn't as good as the previous one. Diego's assessment of beginner's luck had been correct, but I was still two rings from the outer edge of the target.

"You seem to have a flair for this." he commented.

I thanked the many hours, wasted according to my mother, shooting zombies in VR video games as a teen.

We trained for around forty minutes. By that time, my arm

was burning with fatigue. At a little over two pounds, the replica gun was heavy. It was like holding a bag of sugar at arm's length. But we had, at least, progressed to firing multiple rounds in a short burst.

I handed my equipment over and Diego clapped his hand on my shoulder.

"Good start, Jack. The Boss can't complain. You're going to have to come back daily, though. There's still a fair way to go before I let you loose on a real weapon. See you soon, mate."

I left him stowing the gear, and navigated my way back to Doctor Dixon's office.

My basic firearms training had kept my brain occupied for a while but there were still questions I needed to find answers to.

Why had Volkov been to my home? Was he hoping to finish what he had started at the murder scene? Certainly not in human form, unless he had a weapon, or had access to Volsine, to change his shape at will. But, in daylight?

During our telepathic link, he had displayed no hint of a threat. On the contrary, he had been empathetic. I had the impression that he wanted to teach me about the change I was undergoing.

I would probably have to wait another month, to find out.

Doctor Dixon was less patient.

Working with her meant subjecting myself to a battery of tests. Over the next two weeks, she took blood almost daily and scheduled a range of diagnostic scans, ultrasound, x-rays, MRI, CT and Gamma Camera with radioactive dye to highlight organ function.

I spent more time with Sam the physio's workout equipment, pushing myself physically with weights. The Doctor also scheduled several exhausting sessions on a treadmill, connected to

ECG and respiratory monitors, analysing my oxygen uptake and expired gases. I felt like an athlete, training for a high-altitude marathon.

With her encouragement when I excelled, and her chiding when I fell short, I achieved results I could never have anticipated.

We would typically work for half a day, then she would retire to her office, to study the results and pore over the ageing documents delivered by Xander, from Dmitri Alekovic's home. I would head off to the firing range for more coaching from Diego.

Halfway through the second week, she called me into the laboratory, adjoining her office. Despite the punishing physical regime she had been subjecting me to, she looked more tired than I did. I suspected she had been pushing herself as hard as she had been pushing me.

"Jack. Come in, please."

"Hi, Doctor. What do you have planned for me today?"

She pinched her thumb and forefinger together, just above her nose. Spreading them, she smoothed her eyebrows down, then swept the palm of her hand up, over her forehead and backwards over her head, flattening her hair. It was not as precisely arranged as usual, but it was nice to see her appearance a little more relaxed.

"I have a proposal for you." she started, hesitantly. She caught my expression and laughed. "Calm down, Jack. It's not that kind of proposal.

I feigned disappointment, and she continued.

"We've pretty much exhausted all the diagnostic work. The results are good. You're fitter than any human I've ever examined. Your metabolism is in great shape and you have an oxygen uptake and recovery from exercise better than any top-class athlete."

"Good news." I smiled.

Her mock-stern expression indicated the interruption was not appreciated.

"What I'm trying to tell you, Jack, is that you are an extremely healthy human being. But that's as far as it goes. To make any significant progress, I need to examine the Wolf."

"Well, in a couple of weeks . . ." my voice tailed off, as I realised what she was trying to tell me "You've made it, haven't you. The synthetic Volsine. You want to try and force the transformation."

She leaned back in her chair. "Obviously, the final decision lies with you but, at the moment, we can only make any diagnostic observations one night each month. Apart from the fact that it could take me years before I could make any breakthrough at that rate, there's the other matter of a lycanthrope going on a killing spree at the same time."

I didn't need to think. She was doing everything she could to try and fix my situation. Now I had an opportunity to contribute.

"It's okay, Doc. Let's do it"

16

Chapter 16

The testing room had a window, this time. Bullet-proof glass Xander assured me.

There was no reinforced steel door but the chair they had prepared for me owed more to the art of the blacksmith than that of the upholsterer.

Xander gave me a tour of its features.

"Based on estimated measurements from the video of your last transformation, we've fitted titanium steel shackles. There's inflatable padding, to keep them in place as your wrists begin to swell, and they slide in grooves to allow for the lengthening of your forearms. Should keep you secure, without doing you any damage." He beamed with pride over his version of the Inquisitor's chair.

Doctor Dixon was more reassuring,

"We're assuming that Volkov accesses at least part of his human personality whilst transformed, otherwise he would be unable to complete his assassinations and concentrate on a single target. I'm hoping that the purely bestial responses we saw during your last transformation were due to the fact that we had anaesthetised you, putting your conscious mind to sleep, as it were. This time, the theory is that you will remain conscious and, at least partly, in control of the Beast."

I could see she was concerned, so I refrained from commenting that theories and assumptions did little to inspire my confidence, and climbed into the chair.

In preparation, I had stripped off my shirt and was wearing a pair of baggy jogging trousers, with an elasticated waistband. The bare steel of the chair was cold against my exposed back.

Doctor Dixon bolted the manacles and inflated the cuffs to take up the slack. Tying a rubber tourniquet around my upper arm, she deftly inserted a cannula into a vein, and connected an infusion.

She rested a hand on my shoulder and attempted a reassuring smile.

"Are you ready, Jack?" her eyebrows raised.

"Let's get on with it. The suspense is the worst part"

A syringe on the table contained a viscous brown fluid. She connected it to a port on the IV line and quickly but smoothly depressed the plunger until it was empty. Then she was gone, striding out of the door and slamming it behind her.

At first, I felt nothing. Then, as the liquid moved down the IV line and into my arm, I began to feel a warm sensation, radiating from the site of the cannula.

My heart began to accelerate and my mouth became dry. I didn't know whether that was a reaction to the infusion, or simply fear.

The warmth began to spread and intensify, working its way up my arm and into my chest. My heart was pounding like a jack-hammer and I was beginning to panic.

I suddenly realised that I hadn't thought this through. My mind began listing all the ways the procedure could go wrong.

What if the treatment didn't work as the Doctor expected? It could kill me. I could end up stuck in the Wolf form permanently.

Too late, I wished I had pushed my advantage and asked the Doctor for a date. I might not get another chance.

I turned to look at her through the window. She looked up from the displays, showing my vital signs and smiled. If I survived, we definitely needed to have a conversation.

My arms and legs began to twitch involuntarily and the fire in my veins crept up my neck.

Suddenly it hit my brain, my back arched my eyelids opened further than I had thought possible.

It

felt

incredible.

I had assumed, from watching the video, that the process would be painful.

I couldn't have been more wrong.

I thought, is this what it feels like to get high?

I felt as if I were floating, flying.

The clock on the wall opposite suddenly began to recede into the distance at incredible speed. It hovered there, for a moment, as if viewed down the wrong end of a telescope. Then it was hurtling toward me at dizzying velocity, stopping in a nanosecond, exactly where it had started. But now I could see it with crystal clarity. I saw the brush marks, where the wall had been painted and, beneath, tiny irregularities in the surface of the plaster.

My skin tingled. I could feel the hairs growing, thick and coarse, down my forearms, my back, on my face.

As my bones stretched and extended, I felt a euphoric sensation of well-being.

Watching my muscles bulge and expand, I felt energised.

My face extended into a muzzle and my sense of smell multiplied in orders of sensitivity.

I could hear the creaking of the metal under my body.

Fangs erupting from my gums, saliva drowned the dryness in my mouth.

Expanding my barrel chest, each inhalation seemed to take forever, as time slowed to a crawl.

I could hear the ticking of Xander's watch behind the bulletproof glass.

I began to wonder if the hormone had been cut with some mind-expanding substance.

And then I howled.

It was the most natural thing in the world, to throw back my head and celebrate my rebirth in the body of the Wolf.

The sound echoed around the room and I could see the alarm on the faces of Doctor Dixon and Xander, in the next room.

I couldn't help myself.

I howled again, and then I laughed.

That stopped me dead.

The throaty chuckle rattling around the room sounded positively demonic.

Which made me laugh even more.

Once my amusement had run its course, I sat still and looked across at the glass window.

I made no move to free myself. I wanted them to know that I was conscious and rational.

Doctor Dixon leaned forward, and pressed a button on the console in front of her. Her voice sounded tinny on the speaker in my room.

"Mr Allman. Jack. Can you hear me?"

"Eshh."

I hadn't given a thought to any problems with communication, but the muzzle of a Wolf is just not designed to reproduce human speech.

I just hoped she understood. I nodded, to affirm my answer.

"Can you tell me your name?"

"I Chack."

The words were almost lost in a flood of saliva, but she was obviously satisfied, leaving the console and coming back into the room. Xander followed her. I could tell he didn't share her confidence, as he had his hand resting on his holster.

"Chan'r." I tried, laughing at my own ineptitude. He relaxed a little and came closer.

"Damn me, Buddy. Don't you look one hundred percent authentic Anubis."

I nodded.

The Doctor interrogated me further with a few yes/no questions, as it was apparent that normal speech was beyond the capabilities of my current form.

Happy with the results, she toggled a switch on the chair and the manacles clicked open.

Xander took a nervous step back as I rubbed my wrists. I looked at my hands. Instead of paws, as I had half expected, my hands were roughly human in form, but equipped with purposeful-looking curved black claws, about two inches in length.

I leaned forward in the chair, then stepped out on to the floor. To my surprise, I towered over Xander. I knew he was about 6' 2" but I dwarfed him. Hardly surprising he stepped back even further.

Walking felt unnatural. Balancing was difficult. I realised I was, effectively, walking on tiptoe.

I dropped to all fours, feeling instantly more comfortable.

I could sense Xander tensing again. In this stance, I more resembled beast than human. My head was still at the level of his chest

"Oghey Chan'r." I reassured him.

He laughed nervously.

Doctor Dixon was taking it all in her stride.

"Right, Jack. If you would follow me to the diagnostic lab, we can take some blood and get started on some more tests."

She turned on her heel and left the room, without waiting for any acknowledegment.

I pushed past Xander and loped off down the corridor after her, like a pet dog, following its owner. Despite my efforts to reassure him, and the ludicrous image of a wolf wandering down the corridor in jogging pants, I could smell his fear. It was delicious.

The tests I had undergone in my human form proved a little less straightforward in my new shape. Squeezing my massive torso into the MRI scanner was an impossibility. Likewise, ultrasound scanning struggled to penetrate my dense hairy coat. The respiratory function tests were a total non-starter as I found it impossible to grip the mouthpiece in my muzzle.

Even the treadmill presented a challenge as it was barely long enough to accommodate my huge frame, on four legs.

However, I made a mental note to ask Doctor Dixon if she was interested in testing the change in auditory, olfactory and visual perception. In the Wolf form, my scent radar was even more acute. With my eyes closed, I could still see the room, but painted in garish day-glo colours, representing the smells attached to each object. The sharp odour of the alcohol swabs was an electric blue, while the Doctor's skin varied in colour from a cool ivory to a pulsating rose pink.

I could hear the pulse throbbing in her neck and had to fight down the impulse to get closer.

After around an hour of testing, I suddenly began to tire. Stepping off the treadmill, I stood erect and put out a paw to balance myself on the desk. I could feel my senses dulling.

"Jack, are you alright?"

For the first time since the transformation, her professional attitude gave way to concern.

I could still hear her voice, but it sounded flat and distant.

The scent landscape began to fade. I began to panic, it was as if I were going blind.

I was feeling the cold, as the thick pelt receded back into my skin and the creeping weakness as my muscles atrophied before my eyes was terrifying.

"No!" I shouted, and my voice was recognisably human.

I didn't want to go back, to being weak, semi-blind, insignificant.

I began to sob uncontrollably. The gift of a new world of enhanced senses had been snatched away, for now at least.

I felt empty, diminished.

I slid to the floor and sat, hugging my legs to my chest, with my forehead on my knees.

Doctor Dixon threw a blanket around my shoulders and let her arm rest there.

I looked up at her, my cheeks wet. I felt utterly despondent.

She pulled me closer and I let my head drop on to her shoulder.

I shut my eyes and drank in the scent of her. Less vital than it had seemed when I was the Wolf, but still reassuring and safe. My shivering began to subside.

After a few minutes, she relaxed her arm and brushed my hair back from my forehead.

"Go home, Jack. Rest. When you come back tomorrow, we can talk about it."

I nodded, mutely and walked slowly back to collect my clothes.

17

Chapter 17

The moment I opened the door to my apartment, I knew he was there.

While not as acute as in my Wolf-state, my sense of smell alerted me to Volkov's presence.

He looked me up and down.

"You look tired, Jack." He spoke with a pronounced eastern european accent

"What do you want?"

"To talk. Nothing more"

"Why did you come to my apartment, before?"

"To kill you."

"Honest. And now?"

"You were a loose end. My legacy is in your blood. I had to ensure that it did not end up in the wrong hands. I never imagined that you would undergo the Pormena, the transformation. Now it is too late. The cat, as you say, is out of the bag."

"How do I know you won't still try to kill me?"

"You are Wolf-kind now, Vukodlak. We do not kill our own."

"You don't have that problem with humans. You're a serial killer."

"Do not judge me until you know the whole story."

"So tell me."

"Then sit, Jack. This is not a story that is brief in the telling."

He waited until I positioned myself on the sofa, opposite him, then began his tale.

"We lived apart, our tribe. Nomadic. We did not stay too long in any one place but things always ended the same way. Some incident would be blamed on us, and the locals would hunt us down and chase us away.

We were different, and difference breeds fear.

We kept to ourselves, bartered for what we needed. We hunted our food and our needs were simple.

Then the scientists came.

They told us they could make us normal, reintegrate us back into society.

We laughed. Why would we give up our life, our freedom, our beautiful vision of the world? You know of what I speak."

I nodded and he continued.

"They left, or so we thought. But then boys began to go missing.

In Wolf form, the trail was easy to follow, and led us to the research outpost.

We broke in and were outraged by what we found.

They were experimenting on our children!"

His old eyes burned with anger.

"We tried to rescue them, but more of us were captured, and some died. They used tranquiliser darts, and nets of silver wire. There were flamethrowers."

He closed his eyes. I could tell he was reliving a painful memory.

"So we agreed to talk, and their true motives were revealed.

They wanted to use us, to pervert us, to weaponise us. In return for the continued survival of our tribe, they demanded volunteers. They wanted to turn us into assassins. We were virtually unstoppable. Bullets did not harm us and you may already be aware of our regenerative powers."

Involuntarily, my hand strayed to my top lip.

"We refused. The only lives we took were those of the animals we hunted for food.

When they saw we would not cooperate, they found another way to 'deploy' us.

As you already know, if one is unconscious, sedated, when the change takes place, the conscious mind is repressed and the Beast is released."

"How did you......?"

"I felt the Pormena at the full moon, but your personality was absent. What awoke that night was feral, savage.

The military scientists utilised this. Dropping a pack of unconscious Vukodlak on the outskirts of a village, as the full moon rose, was a certain way of ensuring there were few survivors. Our kind were blamed, but it was the military's ethnic cleansing plan which was responsible.

At this point, they were only able to use their captives during the lunar cycle and concentrated their research on the mechanism of the change. They quickly identified Volsine as the hormone responsible and, later located the gland which produced it."

"The Doctor at Vanguard never mentioned that."

"The researchers were kept siloed, working on distinct aspects of the project. Information given to you by Alekovic does not tell the whole story. Those in charge wanted to limit full disclosure to a small elite group.

You may tell your Doctor that the gland lies in the brain, below the pituitary. The Project researchers called it the infrapituitary, in fact. Because of the relative rarity of our kind, whenever it had been previously spotted on a brain scan, it had been dismissed as a mutation, or benign abnormality.

Once they had identified it, they began experimenting in earnest, to find a way to stimulate it, outside the lunar cycle.

The atrocities they committed."

His fists clenched in anger and tears sprang to his red-rimmed eyes.

"Vivisection. Children with electrodes implanted in their brains. Shock therapy. Even removal of the gland, to examine its structure, and attempts to transplant it into non-Vukodlak. Such experiments were invariably fatal.

As was administering Volsine to non-Vukodlak. It seems that, without the receptors required to respond to Volsine in the bloodstream, the subjects suffered multiple organ failure and died in agony. The same happened when the synthetic Volsine was used.

I gather the doctors at Vanguard have successfully reproduced the hormone."

"You felt the, what did you call it, Pormena?"

"Exactly. But I must warn you, Jack. Do not take the synthetic Volsine again."

"Why, are you worried that you won't be able to evade me while I'm in the Wolf-state and you're not"

"No, Jack. Not at all. I advise you for your own benefit. Tell me, how did you feel, as the drug wore off?"

I winced, remembering the crushing depression which had hit me as I was deprived of my enhanced senses and superhuman power.

He read my reaction. "So bad, hm? It will get worse, with each dose, I warn you. The drug is also terribly addictive. Soon you will be in a deep, constant, depression which will worsen until it leads to psychosis. Believe me, I saw it happen too often to my people. Besides, it is not necessary"

"What do you mean?"

He held a wrinkled hand up in front of his face, turned it over and scrutinised the back and the palm in turn.

He closed his eyes and tilted his head slightly, the muscles of his jaw tightening.

As I watched, transfixed, his wrist appeared to grow out of his jacket cuff, sprouting thick grey hair, and his fingers thickened, his nails developing into razor-sharp ebony claws. He flexed and extended his fingers, opened his eyes, and smiled.

"I am old, Jack, and my power is fading. I am unable to achieve a full transformation outside of the lunar cycle. This is why my mission is taking so long. I have to wait for a full month to eliminate each target. But you, you I can show how to change without your synthetic poison."

"What do you want, in return?" I was not going to be recruited into his 'mission' of slaughter.

"From you? Nothing. You are my child, in a way. I am your Predak, your progenitor. I was the last of my kind. Apart from my ongoing task, you are my only legacy. I would see you reach your potential, not be driven mad by meddlers who think they can analyse us like some interesting specimen."

Predak, Father. I felt a twinge of loss for my own Father, but felt connected to this old man in a way I could not explain. He had made me.

I desperately wanted him to teach me how to control the

118

transformation, but I needed to discover his motives and, perhaps, his next target..

"What is your mission. Why are you killing these people? Isn't it a little late for revenge?"

"This has nothing to do with revenge, Jack. Apart from the butchers I dispatched in Europe, do you not wonder why more than one of these scientists resettled in Hope City?"

Even though I had been at two crime scenes in the last month, I had to admit that the relevance of their proximity had gone unnoticed. At least, as far as I was concerned. No doubt the coincidence had not been lost on Agent Simons.

"The chance to start a new life in a new city attracted a lot of immigrants. I just put those two down to coincidence."

"But there are two more, and I fancy my work will not end there."

"Work? What are you talking about? Whatever madness drove you to become a serial killer, Vanguard will find you and stop you. And they're not planning on taking you alive."

I stopped, realising that I had probably revealed too much.

He settled back in his chair.

"Do you have coffee, Jack? There is a second part to my story, and my old throat is very dry."

"Alice, make coffee for two."

"Certainly, Jack"

As the coffee grinder whirred to life, Volkov continued.

"With the coming disintegration of the Yugoslav Republic, funding and support for the Project were to end.

Those in charge decided that it would be better that there be no Vukodlak remaining, that their potential should not be inherited by the government of any of the emerging new countries, giving them a strategic advantage over their neighbours during a period of instability.

The troops roamed the countryside armed with flamethrowers, silver bullets and bayonets. They were aware of our weakness even then."

He touched his face.

"Scars caused by silver never disappear."

He dropped his hand and went on with his story.

"Settlements were destroyed, sometimes on the mere suspicion of harbouring Vukodlak.

Those held in the facility were 'euthanised' and their bodies burned, to destroy evidence."

I handed him his coffee.

"Not all of the technicians in the military labs were inhuman torturers. Many had been pressed into service and had no idea what they were going to be involved in. Some tried to help my people escape but were executed alongside them.

Others, not so brave, remained in touch with me. They would alert me if any information surfaced on the whereabouts of surviving Vukodlak, as a gesture to atone for their guilt. Unfortunately, in every case, either the leads were false or agents of the Secret Police reached my people before I did.

As I said, I was the last.

Then, last year, information reached me that someone was contacting scientists from the Project, recruiting them.

Someone is trying to resurrect the Vukodlak."

He sipped his drink.

"We are of the past, when our gift was considered magic. In this modern world, we have become a scientific curiosity. We have been analysed, dissected, exploited. We have no place. The Vukodlak should be allowed to rest in peace.

This is my mission, to prevent the butchers and torturers from corrupting my legacy. I have to ensure the Vukodlak do not reappear. These abusers too must be wiped from the Earth."

"Perhaps we can help each other."

"What do you suggest?"

"You teach me about the Vukodlak. After all, it's my heritage now. I use my connections within Vanguard to investigate who is recruiting the scientists, and what they are planning. Perhaps we can stop them together."

"Jack. You are too trusting. I cannot trust agents of any Government to do what needs to be done.

However, teach you, that I can do."

Sensing that I had all the information he was willing to share on his 'mission', I dared to press him on the secret of how to transform at will.

"Have you ever meditated?" he asked.

"A little. I tried it after my accident. It helped keep me positive, relaxed"

"Excellent, then we have a head start. Now, relax and close your eyes. Remember how it felt when we communicated during the Pormena."

Relaxing was not easy, knowing that he was sitting opposite me with razor-tipped claws unsheathed, but I shut my eyes and opened my mind.

I felt as if there were an itch, inside my brain. It wasn't as defined as in the Wolf state, but I recognised Volkov's presence. I heard his voice in my mind, as clearly as if he were speaking out loud.

"Good. Now you must visualise the infrapituitary. There is no need to know its true form. Just imagine it as a rubber bulb, or a grape, filled with fluid. Do you see it?"

"I...yes. I think so."

"Now imagine squeezing it, gently, so a little of the fluid is released, inside your head."

I could feel him, in my brain, helping to give form and detail to the image I was creating, making it sharper and more defined. I tried to imagine the bulb squeezing, but the mental image remained rigid.

"Don't try too hard, Jack. You have to relate the image to the result you desire. Let's try to imagine the properties of the Volsine, how it makes you feel. The power, the pleasure."

That was the key. My heart rate began to accelerate, and the familiar warmth began to infuse my head.

"Relax, Jack. Take control. We are not aiming for a total Pormena. Focus on the part of the body you wish to transform. Feel the receptors in that area absorbing the Volsine, and the tissues reacting."

I tried to concentrate on my hands, as he had done, but the fire in my blood had already reached my face, so I tried to slow the progress.

I opened my eyes, just in time to see the hairy muzzle sprouting just below them. I could feel the fangs erupting from my gums, and my brain translated the signals from my hypersensitive nose into a multicoloured scentscape.

There were so many sounds. In the quiet of the Vanguard labs, hypersensitive hearing had not been a problem. In an apartment, overlooking a busy road, with other people living above, below and around me, the incidental noise was decidedly uncomfortable.

I could hear washing machines, the cooling fans in the Taxees across the street, as they charged wirelessly from the inductive couplings buried in the tarmac beneath their parking bays. And...

something else.

It sounded like someone cocking a gun, at least from what I'd seen on TV and there were distorted voices and static, as if on walkie-talkies.

I panicked. I needed to warn Volkov, but I couldn't speak with my distorted face. I desperately tried to concentrate, to speak to his mind as he had spoken to mine.

"Don't panic, Jack. You will be able to control the extent and duration of the change, with practice."

I shook my head frantically, pointing towards the door, which suddenly exploded inwards, in a cloud of smoke.

The concussion overwhelmed my newly-enhanced hearing and I was rendered virtually deaf. The acrid smell of the explosives blanketed the scentscape in a dirty brown. Struggling to regain control of my mouth, I turned to look at Volkov. He had not moved from his chair. There was a resigned expression on his face, which now looked tired and very old, and rather incongruous, with the green dots of three laser sights centred on his forehead.

In my head, I heard "Let it end. Promise me. No more Vukodlak."

Outside, I could hear nothing, but he mouthed "It's all right, Jack."

Through the clamorous ringing in my ears, I faintly perceived three rapid cracks, accompanied by three flashes in the smoke, and Volkov's chair tipped over backwards, hitting the floor heavily.

Before I could stand, the bullets were followed by three armed men in tactical armour. Standing over the body, one of them was speaking into a microphone. His voice, to me, was still muffled.

There was a hand on my shoulder. I swivelled my head slowly, to find myself looking at Xander. I could tell he was saying my name.

Stunned by the speed and violence of what had happened, I allowed him to pull me to my feet and lead me down the stairs to the street, into a windowless black van waiting at the kerb.

As the van slid soundlessly away from the apartment block, my hearing was beginning to return.

"Sorry, " started Xander.

I didn't want to hear his apologies.

"For what?" I retorted. "For executing an old man in my apartment?"

"I was going to say, for taking so long to get there. It takes time to get a TAC team together."

"He was unarmed, Xander. There was no need to kill him."

"He was a serial killing Werewolf. He was a weapon in himself. I was trying to save your life. If that was at the expense of his, so be it."

I burned with anger and a loss I couldn't explain.

No, there was no justification. He had not been there to harm me. He had come to teach me, to be my mentor.

He had been my Predak, my family. And now, like all the rest, he was gone.

We didn't speak for the duration of the journey back to Vanguard.

18

Chapter 18

When we arrived at Vanguard, we went our separate ways. I assumed Xander had gone to report to Simons.

Doctor Dixon was waiting for me in the common area, quiet at that time of night. Concern was clear on her face.

"Jack. Are you hurt?" She put a hand on my upper arm.

"No, Doc. I'm fine. A slight buzzing in the ears after the explosion, but it's clearing."

"Sit, please. I'll fetch coffee."

Coming back, she sat beside me. "I'm sorry about what happened."

"Seems everyone is, but that didn't stop it happening. They murdered that old man in my home."

My mind was in turmoil, seething with rage, paralysed by loss.

Despite the knowledge that Volkov was a serial killer, I felt a profound sense of emptiness, knowing he was gone.

We had shared a psychic link. We had been connected at the moment of his death. I didn't just see him die. I felt his passing, like a bright beacon suddenly being extinguished.

He was the only person who truly understood my condition. He had been on the threshold of teaching me more about my abilities and now he was dead. I was alone. Worse, he was my Predak. I had just become an orphan for the second time

I couldn't explain that to anyone at Vanguard.

I realised that they must still have been monitoring me. After such a breach of trust and the butchery I'd just witnessed, I was not in a hurry to share what I had learnt.

All I had to show the Doctor were my anger and disgust.

Despite my treating her approach with disdain, she handed me the coffee and sat beside me, her hand on my arm.

"I can't make excuses for what happened, Jack, but please know that I have nothing to do with operational matters. I'm here if you need to talk, if you need to get it off your chest. I can't imagine how you feel.

Just so you know, I don't just regard you as a patient. I'd hoped we were friends too."

She took a sip of her own drink, the steam clouding her glasses.

As she took them off to clean them, my anger dissipated. She was right. None of this was her fault and she had always treated me as a person first and a patient second.

"No, Doc. I'm sorry. I shouldn't have snapped at you for what Xander did. I've never actually witnessed a death before. And in my home. It's like a surreal bad dream."

"Call me Annie.." she smiled.

"Not Dixie?"

"Excuse me?"

I realised my mistake too late, and tried to back-pedal.

"Oh, it was just that was Xander called you. I wondered if you two were . ."

She raised an eyebrow and pursed her lips. I left the question unasked.

Seeing my embarrassment, she grinned widely and patted my

arm.

"Agent Walters is an attractive man, and we have been out for a drink, once. He was a perfect gentleman. However, we have some fundamental differences in ideology which prevent us from being anything other than friends."

Now I was the one raising an eyebrow, and she continued.

"For instance, what happened in your apartment. I'm afraid I don't see such situations in the same black and white manner as some others at Vanguard. I'm a physician and, for me, National Security does not trump the sanctity of a human life. The end does not always justify the means."

"Then why stay?"

"A lot of the time it's not like that. I have a chance to do good. As you may have guessed, we deal with cases which lie outside the purview of regular law enforcement. I have seen incredible things.

Yours isn't the first transformation I've witnessed."

That surprised me.

"Agents brought in a man, two years ago, who could change his facial features at will. He could become anyone he wanted to be. It was an amazing ability but, when we met, he was almost suicidal."

"Why?"

"He'd been changing his face since he was a child. To escape abusers, to hide after he was forced to steal to eat. He'd spent so much time living with other people's faces, he didn't know what his own looked like. He felt as if he had no identity of his own."

"What happened to him?" I feared the worst.

"We created him a face?"

"How?"

127

"He could recall his face as a child but, when he showed us, it looked totally out of place on an adult body. We used software to create a predictive image of what he should look like at his current age, and built a three-dimensional model. After studying it, he was able to copy it. He now has his own unique face, his own identity.

After that, he was recruited. He's currently somewhere in Eastern Europe, gathering intelligence. The perfect undercover agent."

I could see the pride she felt for a job well done, and a broken life repaired.

"How did you ever come to be working for an organisation like Vanguard."

"My Father was an Agent. I didn't know. I was working in medical research, in London, when I got a call telling me he was seriously ill. That was my first introduction to Vanguard. I thought he was just a civil servant."

"He was ill?"

"That was all I was told, initially. He was being treated in the old Vanguard headquarters. When I arrived, I discovered the whole story. He'd been bitten by a venomous Scincomorph."

"A what?"

"A Saurian. A Lizard Man."

I stared, open-mouthed.

But, why not? If Werewolves existed, why not Lizard Men?

She laughed at my expression.

"You thought you were the only undiscovered species on the planet?"

"Sorry. It's just...Anyway, your Father."

"Because of my background, I was allowed to work with the Vanguard scientists. To be honest, the organisation was still in its infancy, and they had very little clue on how to treat him. Together, we began to make some progress. Eventually, we developed an antitoxin.

Unfortunately, it was too late to help my Father."

"I'm sorry, Annie."

"It was a long time ago. It's been a while since I told anyone about it."

She stopped and her expression changed. She quickly removed her hand from my arm.

She was looking past me, over my shoulder.

I turned, to see Xander in the office doorway, his face expressionless.

"Simons wants to see you."

I followed him down the corridor in silence.

My irritation at his untimely appearance reignited the flames of my anger.

I wanted to hit him. Apart from the cold-blooded murder he had just sanctioned in my apartment, I realised that I'd been deceived. All the talk of being a useful asset, an Agent, was rubbish. They were still watching me. They had used me as bait to get to Volkov.

Xander knocked on the door to Simons' office and entered.

Simons was scrutinising an image of my apartment on his wallscreen, the armchair on its back, bloodstains on the wall behind.

"Thank you, Agent Walters. Please close the door on your way out.

Jack, take a seat.

I deeply regret the way this business has been concluded."

I didn't believe a word.

"You got your result. The serial killer is dead. No trial. No awkward explanations. No external witnesses. All tidied up.

Except for the fact that you blew the door off my apartment and murdered an unarmed man in the middle of my lounge."

"I understand your bitterness Jack and, for what it's worth, I do believe Walters could have handled things better. Termination may not have been the only option."

"Well, it's a little late now." Bitterness? That was an understatement.

I couldn't hold back my frustration.

"How did he know Volkov was there? You're still having me followed, aren't you?"

"Believe it or not, no. Volkov had been to your home before. It was not unreasonable to suspect that he might return. Leaving a fly-on-the-wall surveillance bug across the street seemed a sensible precaution."

"Oh." my righteous indignation was summarily deflated. Reluctantly, I had to agree.

Simons was straight to the point.

"So. What did he want?"

"He came to explain his motives."

He frowned.

"To you? Why?"

"I'm not sure. He didn't try to justify the killings, but he told me why he committed them. I don't know if he was looking for an ally, or just wanted someone to know his side of the story."

"I'm all ears. This has been an unusual case, to say the least. And you have the advantage of seeing inside the mind of a serial killer, literally."

I related Volkov's tale to Simons, who listened in silence.

I included his warning about the use of synthetic Volsine,

but refrained from mentioning the possibility of a non-lunar transformation.

I still felt that Vanguard had betrayed my trust and was concerned about how they would react to the revelation that I might have additional abilities.

When I finished the story, Simons steepled his fingers in front of his face and pursed his lips.

"Volkov didn't name the person trying to recruit the scientists?"

"He might have if he'd had more time." I retorted.

"Quite. I take it he didn't mention the other party's motives, or their location?"

"I'm not sure he had uncovered their plan, apart from the exploitation of the Vukodlak for personal gain, which is why he was so determined to eliminate them. As to location, with at least two of them relocating to Hope City, and he mentioned two more, I can only assume this new player is local."

"I'd say that was a valid assumption, Mr Allman. I'll leave you to return to Doctor Dixon's care. Could you send Walters in, on your way out?

Oh, by the way, I've dispatched a clean-up crew to your apartment. Sorry for the inconvenience."

The next couple of weeks seemed interminable.

Annie was horrified when I shared Volkov's revelation about the side-effects of the synthetic Volsine. We both agreed that I would not be repeating the experiment.

She wanted to begin a thorough physical and mental assessment, to determine if she had already done any harm. I convinced her that it was unnecessary.

I assured her I felt fine, and I did.

Simons had me trawling through months worth of communications between Alekovic and his colleagues, looking for any clue as to who had called on the skills of the ex-Yugoslav scientists. There was nothing. Nor was there any mention of what their aim might be.

If, as Volkov had suspected, it was another attempt to weaponise Vukodlak, then I was likely to be a target. For that reason, I was being kept busy in the office, while Xander did the field work.

Each afternoon, I dutifully attended the firing range, where Diego continued to hone my skills. My aim was improving, and he now had me stripping a real weapon and fixing common faults. He was a patient, but exacting, tutor.

Initially, I found it rather incongruous that a man whose stock in trade was instruments of death should be so obsessed with safety. He shared his philosophy with me. According to Diego, the most dangerous part of the gun was the hand holding it. If he could exert some degree of influence over the hand, he hoped to prevent misuse of the weapon. I couldn't argue.

Every night, I tried to repeat the self-stimulation of the infrapituitary as Volkov had shown me. For several days my efforts resulted only in failure and a pounding headache.

At the beginning of the second week, however, I began to make progress.

To begin with, I could muster only a faint warmth inside my skull and was rewarded with the faintly obscene sight of an extended hairy middle finger. As the full moon drew closer my confidence and my ability grew to the extent that I was able to transform the whole of my left arm.

The complete Pormena still eluded me.

In a couple of nights, I wouldn't need to try.

Simons' investigation of the plot Volkov had revealed was meeting with even less success. He had been unable to find anything in the background of any of the dead scientists which might suggest a recent link between them. Once informed of the death of Volkov, Milena Alekovic rejected any further approaches from Vanguard. There were no further leads.

The atmosphere between me and Xander had thawed.

I accepted his explanation that he believed my life was in danger, but I still found it hard to associate this cold killer with my boyhood friend. Ironically, I found it easier to accept that I had become a Werewolf.

On the night of the full moon, we all gathered in the room with the steel chair.

There was no need for restraints, but it was the only place I could comfortably sit during the Pormena.

When it began, I could immediately discern a difference between the natural change and that initiated by the synthetic Volsine. The onset was slower and more relaxed. The feeling of incredible vitality and well-being flowed gently across my body in a wave, rather than hitting me like a tsunami. I settled back into the chair, relishing the steady sharpening of my senses, picking out new sounds and scents, as my body mass swelled with the hypertrophy of muscle.

The enjoyment of the moment was marred by a sense of loss. There would be no link with my Predak.

But there was another.

I sat up, suddenly, in the chair.

Xander, beside me, spilled his coffee as he retreated in alarm.

I closed my eyes and searched with my mind, trying to focus

on the presence.

Fear, panic, escape.

The feelings were unclear, jumbled, and I couldn't tell if the other Vukodlak was aware of me.

In my excitement, I tried to communicate with my colleagues. "Woof."

Xander laughed "Dog impressions, Nube?"

I shook my head "Woowf." and pointed to myself.

He looked confused "Yes, you're a Wolf. And?"

I pointed off into the distance and repeated myself.

Simons pushed to the front "Wolf? Another Wolf, Jack?"

I pointed at him and nodded, vigorously.

"Where? Can you tell?"

I shrugged my shoulders.

Simons began an animated conversation with Xander.

"Another Wolf? An accomplice, or related to the scientists' new employer?"

I was not listening. The Other's emotions were changing. Confidence, power, violence.

I felt, rather than saw, him kill his first victim. A swing of those vicious claws, and it was over. Then another fell prey to his new-found lethal abilities. Now there was excitement, pleasure, but a need to escape. He ran.

My link to the new Vukodlak was not as strong as that I had had with Volkov. I attributed it to my lack of experience but continued trying to communicate.

I had a faint impression that he was aware of my presence. I tried to send feelings of empathy, understanding, trust.

The image I received in return was unclear, out of focus. He was standing in front of a shop window, on all fours, looking at his reflection.

I could feel his excitement, exhilaration.

He was a lean beast, with huge shoulders and an intense red pelt.

I knew who he was!

The horror of my realisation must have transmitted to him. He withdrew his cooperation, trust instantly shattered, and the connection was broken.

I was still aware of his existence but I couldn't reconnect.

I howled in frustration.

Simons, uncowed, put his hand on my arm.

"Jack. What's wrong?"

I waved my hands over my head "Ngong."

"The other Wolf?"

I nodded, mutely.

In my current form, there was no way I could tell them my guilty secret.

I had created a monster.

Before night turned into dawn, my secret was out.

Simons' phone rang and he stepped into the corridor to answer it.

The concern was clear to see when he returned.

"There's been an incident at New Armley."

The prison had been named after the original Armley jail. It had been obliterated, along with its unfortunate occupants, during the meteor strike which erased the rest of the city of Leeds. The new prison had been built on the outskirts of the city, near to the new Motorway Link.

He looked me in the face.

"You know, don't you?"

I nodded, and hung my head.

Xander had no idea what was happening.

"He knows? What."

Simons' reply was to log in to a computer terminal in the anteroom and open a video file.

We gathered around to watch.

The image was of a corridor, obviously in the jail, with doors down either side.

As we watched, two guards entered the frame. They stood, talking, outside one of the doors. It was an animated conversation. Although there was no audio, it was clear that they were arguing.

They appeared to listen at the door. One of them pressed a button, on an intercom, beside it. He spoke into the microphone but, apparently, could make no sense of the reply.

Standing back from the door, they unholstered their taser pistols and waved an access card in front of the electronic lock.

A massive red bulk launched itself through the open doorway, swinging its claws with murderous accuracy. One of the guards fell, clutching his throat, in an attempt to stem the bleeding. His colleague fired his taser.

The monster didn't even seem to notice, almost decapitating the second guard with a single strike.

It then turned, and headed off down the corridor.

It was all over in seconds.

Simons stopped the playback .

"The little thug that Jack bit, Dylan Myers, just turned into a Wolf. He killed two guards, and escaped."

"But Jack hadn't even become a Wolf when he bit him." protested Xander.

"True." agreed Annie, "But the infection was in his system. It must have passed in his saliva. What are the odds, given the rarity of those carrying the Vukodlak gene?"

"Yes, fascinating." countered Simons. "I'm not a gambling man, but I'm betting we've not seen the last of this character.

Walters, you need to go to the jail, immediately. Give them a cover story. Myers made a weapon from cutlery, or somebody smuggled one in, something along those lines. And make sure that CCTV footage disappears. I'll put an alert out for Dylan Myers."

They left the room, together.

I sat heavily in the chair.

Annie came to my side, one hand on my shoulder, and held my paw with the other.

"It's not your fault, Jack. You couldn't know. The chances were minute."

I shook my head, ashamed. It felt like my fault.

She slid her hand from my shoulder, down to my forearm, and rested her head against my chest.

She was still there, when the Pormena came to an end.

19

Chapter 19

I'd felt guilty about Hedoen Volkov's death. After all, he had been ambushed coming to see me, and was executed in my apartment.

But that was nothing compared to the anguish I felt following Dylan Myers' escape.

I had unleashed the beast. My actions had turned him into the murderous animal which had taken the lives of two prison guards.

No matter how much Annie and Xander tried to reassure me that it was not my fault, I felt responsible.

I needed to make amends.

The next day, and each subsequent day, I was in Simons' office. I knew my record searching was a futile task, calculated to keep me busy, and out of the way. There wasn't even any proof of criminal activity, unlike the Dylan Myers case.

I pestered him to let me go out in the field with Xander, to do something more useful. As I pointed out, I'd be in the company of one of his most trusted Agents. What could go wrong?

So, when Xander burst into the office, announcing that one of Myers' known associates had been spotted by a public safety drone, I insisted on accompanying him. Simons reluctantly capitulated.

We sped out of the underground car park in one of Vanguard's manual-drive electric cars, weaving in and out of brightly coloured Taxees, across town to a low-rent residential area.

Our target had been spotted in a local garage and Vanguard had hijacked the drone, to follow him at a distance.

We caught up with him, in an alley between two apartment blocks in the company of two other youths.

Xander flashed his Vanguard badge and ordered the other two to get lost.

I'm sure they never even looked at the I.D. but Xander's demeanour screamed Law loud enough for them to leave without an argument.

He turned his attention to the remaining teenager.

Standing around 5'5" in his trainers, the kid was overweight and shabbily dressed. His blonde hair was badly in need of a wash. The acrid stench of body odour assailed my hypersensitive nose, already suffering the unidentifiable miasma of aromas emanating from a nearby dumpster. .

He leant against the wall, eyeing Xander up and down. He was trying to look confident, but fooling no-one.

Xander took a step closer and spoke quietly.

"Boris."

"Who wants to know?"

"Someone who's looking for Dylan Myers."

"Well, you're looking in the wrong place. He's in New Armley."

"Not since last night. Have you seen him?"

"I didn't go visit, if that's what you mean."

"Listen, kid. He killed two people. He's dangerous and possibly armed and we want him off the street. If you hear from him, you let us know. OK?"

"That's what the other guy said. How much are you offering?"

"Other guy?"

"Yeah. Old geezer. Flash car he had. Well sporty. Offered me £250. What've you got?"

Xander peeled back his overcoat to reveal his holstered taser pistol. "This."

"Yeah. Right."

The kid's eyes flicked between the taser and Xander's face, uncertain whether to take the threat seriously. He swallowed, nervously.

"The other guy gave me £50 up front, to call him first. A...a...sign of good faith, he called it. A down payment, like."

Xander drew the pistol.

"Do you have his name?"

"No. He just left me a number to call if Dill turned up."

Xander pulled the trigger gently, and the barbed electrodes leapt from the pistol and embedded themselves in Boris's tatty denim jacket.

"Would you like to give me the number?"

The boy was sweating by this time, fishing frantically in his pocket to find the scrap of paper which he surrendered to Xander.

Xander gave him a card in return.

"If Dylan contacts you, call that number, immediately."

His face was inches from that of the frightened youth, when he pulled the trigger.

He waited, impassively, until his victim had stopped twitching. Stepping carefully, to avoid the pool of fresh urine, he unhooked the taser barbs from the kid's jacket.

"Consider that MY down payment," he hissed. "and there's more where that came from if you double-cross me."

He looked at me and nodded with his head to signal that I should return to the car.

I was frozen, aghast at the casual brutality I had witnessed. I was finding it more and more difficult to reconcile this side of Xander's character with the happy-go-lucky schoolfriend I remembered.

Several days had passed since our encounter with Boris, but Dylan Myers still eluded all attempts to locate him.

Agent Simons was baffled. As he put it "I would have expected someone with this young man's intellectual deficit to be more demonstrative of his new physical prowess."

I think he had expected Dylan to embark on a one-man crime wave.

The only unusual activity was the disappearance of several homeless people. Simons was of the opinion that there was no connection to Myers.

"Unless he's eating them." smirked Xander

"Sometimes, Agent Walters, your sense of humour leaves much to be desired." was Simons' terse response.

I had tried to focus on a mental link with Dylan, but he managed to elude me.

The search was at a standstill.

I wasn't complaining. I'd had a chance to spend some more time with Annie. We discovered more common ground than we expected. Apart from losing our parents in extraordinary circumstances, we shared tastes in music and cuisine. I'd never met a woman before who liked classic rock AND tapas.

She was a very good listener and, since my first encounter with Hedoen Volkov, I had quite a tale to tell.

Sharing my fears and uncertainties had helped to put things

into proportion. Although she continued her efforts to find a 'cure', I was no longer sure that I wanted one. Initially, I had considered my lycanthropy an affliction. It had already brought me tears and misery. But it had also brought me strength and a sense of uniqueness I had been lacking. Yes, I was a freak, but I was coming to terms with it. Although I had vowed not to be caught up in Volkov's web of murder, I felt an obligation to find out what lay behind the mystery. After all, I was one of the last Vukodlak.

Simons told me just as much as he thought I needed to know, and Xander had changed so much in the years since we last met, that I no longer felt comfortable confiding in him.

Annie, I felt I could trust.

So it was with her that I shared my secret.

My nightly practising had gone well and I could now transform most of my upper body, at will.

I wasn't sure what was holding me back from achieving a total metamorphosis. I hoped that sharing the secret with someone who would give me encouragement might help.

I found her alone in her office, walked in and close the door behind me.

"Annie, I have something to show you."

She looked up from notes.

"What is it, Jack? You look very serious."

"I haven't told anyone else about this."

She smiled, nervously.

"Come on, Jack You're worrying me."

I held my arm out across her desk, closed my eyes and tried to focus on the Pormena.

Seconds passed.

Nothing.

"Jack?"

I opened my eyes.

"Sorry, I don't normally have a problem with performance anxiety."

She cocked her head to one side and looked at me smiling, expectantly.

"Good to know, but…"

And there it was. All it took was a smile to relax me, and the warm flush travelled from my brain, down into my arms.

As my shirt sleeves bulged, and began to split at the seams, I realised I had not really thought this through.

Coarse black hair covered my forearms and my magnified hands sprouted ebony claws.

Her eyes widened.

No, I thought, don't let me frighten her.

But she was grinning. Like a child seeing Santa Claus for the first time.

"Jack. That's amazing. How..?"

I explained how Volkov had imparted his secret, just before his death.

Her expression changed to concern.

"Did anyone on the TAC Team see you?"

To be honest, I hadn't even considered that possibility, but I was fairly certain that I had returned almost to normal before they stormed my apartment.

"I don't think so."

"Good. But we have to tell Simons."

I was hesitant.

"I'm not sure I trust him. I never know what he's thinking."

"I hope you trust me?"

"Why else would I show you?"

"Thank you, Jack. That means a lot. Now, listen. I trust Simons with my life. He needs to know."

"Okay."

"Wait here. I'll see if he's in."

Rather than wait, I poked my head out of the office door. Satisfied that there was no-one about, I walked quickly back to the room where I had left my jacket and put it back on, to hide my ruined shirtsleeves.

I was on my way back to Annie's office when Xander caught me.

"Nube. Good news. Boris just confirmed he has a meeting with Dylan Myers."

"He rang?" I was surprised. "Must be because you asked so nicely."

Xander ignored the irony

"I can't find Simons and could use an extra pair of hands. You good?"

"Well, I . ."

"C'mon. It's happening now. We can't afford to lose him. I've called TAC, but they won't be ready in time."

This was the first lead we'd had on Dylan's whereabouts.

The telephone number Boris had given Xander was an untraceable mobile and had been a dead end. This was our first real break.

I reluctantly agreed. I hoped I might, at least, be able to save Dylan from the same fate as Volkov.

20

Chapter 20

It was dark by the time we reached our destination.

Part of the industrial area of the new city lay on the River Aire, which had once run through the centre of Leeds.

Now it served as a thoroughfare for automated barges, the water-borne equivalent of the Taxees.

Xander's information took us to a warehouse by the waterside.

I could see no-one about as we approached the squat building. As most warehousing functions were now carried out by drones and bots, human involvement was mainly limited to security.

The watchman's hut was empty. Xander drew his pistol. Not a taser, on this occasion.

I put my hand on his shoulder and motioned him to stop.

Closing my eyes, I listened intently. Inhaling, I scanned the scentscape.

No-one was moving in the building, but I could identify at least eight different human trails.

What I couldn't tell was how old they were. Frustrated, I whispered to Xander.

"I can't tell how many there are, but they're keeping very quiet. Are you sure this isn't a trap?"

"It's possible, but I don't think Myers is that clever. Besides, he doesn't know I've got my JackalMan with me."

He grinned and edged his way closer to the door.

Pressing his ear to the metal surface, he slowly turned the handle.

The door opened, soundlessly, and he stepped inside.

Just beyond the door, a stack of crates provided cover and he squatted behind them, signalling me to follow.

Following the line of crates, we made our way to the side wall of the warehouse, hidden from sight.

From there, I could clearly identify two scents.

One was Boris.

The other, unknown, smelled lightly of soap and expensive aftershave.

It was not Dylan.

Something was wrong. I turned to alert Xander, but collided with one of the crates.

A voice spoke from the centre of the floor.

"Good evening, Mr Allman. Please come out. We've been expecting you."

I heard a click, as Xander cocked his gun, and braced myself for the firefight to come.

But he was pointing it at me.

I raised my hands, unsure what to do next.

"Xander?"

He waved the gun, indicating I should come out from behind the crates.

I stepped into the light.

Boris was standing behind a tall man, of around seventy. His thinning white hair was combed back from his high forehead, curiously at odds with his thick black eyebrows.

"Agent Walters. Good evening. Thank you for bringing our guest."

It WAS a trap, but Xander was not the intended prey.

"Mr Allman. A pleasure to meet you at last. Allow me to introduce myself. My name is Ambrose Pearse."

He extended a thin hand and tilted his head to one side like a bird of prey studying a mouse.

Unsure what else to do, I took the hand and shook it. It was cold, but the grip was strong.

He turned to Xander. "Thank you, Agent. I will contact you shortly to conclude our arrangement."

Xander nodded. I realised I had been right. This was no longer the Alexander Walters I had known as a boy.

"Xander. Why?"

"There are things you don't understand yet, Jack. Things outside your self-absorbed little bubble. You can go with the flow, or against it. You're not human anymore. You're a freak, an abomination. This is where you belong, not with decent folks."

"Annie, you mean?"

"You're not good for her, Jack. You're tainted. She deserves better. Did you know she wants to have kids, eventually? What can you give her, a litter of wolf cubs?"

"Better? You mean, like you?" I could feel the anger at his betrayal boiling up inside me. I clenched my fists. "I ought to..."

He pointed at my hands.

"There you go, Buddy. Made my point. You have a nasty temper to go with those sharp teeth. What happens if, one day, she upsets you? You going to bite her too?

You've already spread your infection, and I'm going to have to clean up after you. Sorry it happened to you, Jack. If Dixie

147

misses you, I'll buy her a puppy. It was nice to see a face from the old days. For a while, at least. Be seeing you. Or not."

He clapped me on the shoulder.

Looking past me, he smirked "Bye, Boris."

"You tasered me, you bastard." Boris whined. "That wasn't part of the deal. I pissed myself."

"Had to make it look real, kid. No hard feelings."

Holstering his pistol, he turned and left.

Pearse had watched the exchange with his hands clasped in front of him. Now he reached inside his black overcoat and produced a gold pocket watch.

He flicked the case open and looked at the dial.

"Almost dinner time, Mr Allman. I do hope you'll join me?"

"Do I have a choice?"

He raised his hand to the level of his right shoulder and snapped his fingers.

Six men in body armour stepped out of the shadows, four of them holding batons.

The recent scent trails I had sensed earlier.

They activated their batons. There was a hum and a light blue aurora formed around the tip of each one. Stun sticks. I'd seen them used for crowd control in some South American countries, where rapid restoration of order was rated more important than human rights. A touch to the skull was like a taser to the brain, but they tended to be wielded with more force. Physical damage often ensued.

I was betrayed and alone. There was nothing to gain by being beaten unconscious as well

I decided to bide my time, and see what was on the menu for dinner.

The plush company limousine came to a halt outside a four-storey building.

The majority of the facade was clad in black glass. Atop the fourth floor, a neon sign displayed the name 'Novo Lupus Biotechnologies'

Mr Pearse was either not as shy about his operation as Vanguard or I was in a situation with two possible outcomes.

I doubted one of them would be pleasant.

A roller shutter pulled up, to give access to an underground car park.

Pearse had ridden in the front with the chauffeur, leaving me locked in the back, with my thoughts.

I couldn't fathom Xander's motives. Was it about money? Did he really think I was only fit to be experimented on? I assumed that was Pearse's intention. Or was Xander really so jealous of the warming relationship between Annie and me that he would do anything to have me out of the picture?

At any rate, I was on my own again. It wasn't an unfamiliar situation for me but, even without a pack, this Wolf wasn't about to suffer Fate's latest abuse without a fight. I'd pretty much had enough of being thrown from crisis to drama and back. It was time to take positive action. I just had to be on the lookout for an opportunity.

The driver opened my door and indicated an airport-style detector arch beside the lift.

As I passed through, red lights began to flash and the alarm sounded.

Pearse smiled, and held out an open metal case.

"I must ask that you hand over any mobile devices, your watch and your vglasses please, Jack. The back of the car, and this garage level are shielded against transmission, but I cannot take

149

the risk of recordings being made inside the laboratory complex. The World will know of our work soon enough, but I reserve the right to control the timetable."

I handed them over, as requested. My second pass through the arch was rewarded with silence.

The interior of the elevator was painted cream and there were leather-upholstered benches on the side walls.

A seam up the rear wall indicated a second pair of doors, and I noticed that the control panel showed more floors below ground than above.

At least two of them required keycard access.

The front pair of lift doors opened on to the third floor. The space before me was as opulent as any hotel I had ever seen.

A huge wooden desk backed on to the front-facing window, with a deep buttoned leather swivel chair behind.

Across one long wall a bookcase looked down on two red leather armchairs and a matching three-seater sofa, clustered around a low table.

On the other side of the room, looking a little out of place in an office setting, was a four-seater dining table, with places set for two.

Pearse pulled down the fake spines of a row of books, to reveal several glasses and decanters.

"Drink?" he asked.

I declined and stood in the middle of the deep-pile grey carpet, waiting.

He indicated the armchairs.

"Please, Jack. Don't stand on ceremony. Sit. Dinner won't be long. I notified the chef we were on our way."

Settling into one of the chairs, I sat in silence, allowing him to lead the conversation.

"Are you not curious about why you're here, Jack?"

"I'm guessing you're the person responsible for recruiting the Yugoslav scientists. You want to use the Vukodlak, as they tried to, back in the 90's"

"Vukodlak. I detest that word. It conjures images of fear and superstition, pitchforks and flaming torches.

I prefer Homo Lupus. A little pretentious, granted, but a more scientific title.

You are correct, we recruited the Yugoslavs, to assist in our research.

Your friend Mr. Volkov has significantly depleted their numbers, but we have the data we needed.

But, no. I have no intention of weaponising the Wolves."

I raised an eyebrow. "Then what?"

"At the risk of sounding like a cartoon character, Jack, I want to be like you."

I frowned, confused.

"Oh, not the claws, teeth and fur coat. Although there could be some amusement to be had there. No, Jack. I want to live to be over two hundred years old."

Ever since Volkov's revelations about the attempts to use Wolfkind as a military resource, I had not given a thought to the other possible advantages of being a lycanthrope.

"Unfortunately," continued Pearse, "Nature did not bless me with your genetic advantages. So I have turned to science to unravel the secrets of Homo Lupus."

"I founded this company over thirty years ago, as a subsidiary of Pearse Consolidated. We have invested a great deal of time and money, chasing the twin Holy Grails of Biotechnology. Medical Nanobots and Telomere extension."

"Telomeres?" I had no idea what he was talking about.

"Putting it simply,Telomeres are what stop your chromo-somes fraying at the ends. Each time a chromosome replicates, the Telomeres shorten. The average lifespan of the Telomeres varies from fifty to seventy divisions. Once they are gone, the end of the chromosome becomes damaged and it can no longer replicate. That is part of the process of aging. We hope to halt, or even reverse that process."

He held his glass up to the light, and examined the contents.

"We have made great leaps forward with our research, and expect to be able to offer longevity enhancing treatments within the next ten to fifteen years.

Unfortunately, as things stand, I am unlikely to see it."

He took a sip from his drink.

"We have something in common, you and I.

I was also unfortunate enough to be involved in a road acci-dent.

Mine was my own fault."

He smiled, wryly.

"I was born into an age where personal vehicular transport was much more accessible. My teenage passion was for vintage motorcycles.

Unfortunately, there are now very few countries which permit petrol vehicles to be ridden in the way they were intended. An advantage of my business success is that I can afford to transport my bikes to these countries and indulge my vice.

A disadvantage of riding in less-developed countries, how-ever, is that neither the road surfaces nor the local medical facilities are of a standard which would be considered acceptable elsewhere.

The shortcomings of the first left me at the mercy of the

shortcomings of the second. I took a rather nasty tumble, which left both my helmet and my skull in less than optimum condition.

My injuries were such that intervention was required immediately. There was no time to wait until my personal medical team could be flown in.

Following cranial surgery, I was left with a discontinuity in the dura, the membrane which covers the brain.

The surgeons filled the void with donor tissue and I made a full recovery."

He paused, touching his head, just above the left temple. A white scar traced an arc backwards, over his ear.

"Sadly, the local medical team which carried out the procedure was unaware of a condition called iCJD, or acquired Prion disease, which can be transmitted via infected tissue.

The donor cadaver carried the infection, but their pre-harvesting analysis did not detect it.

I now find myself showing early signs of a degenerative neurological disorder and, while new protein-blocking drugs we have developed slow the progress, I have a severely limited life-expectancy."

I began to see the motive driving his research. "You're hoping that becoming Vukodlak will cure you."

"The Homo Lupus programme is not the only avenue we have explored. Just as Werewolves have long been the subject of myth, other legends purporting to provide clues to longevity and a cure for all ills have circulated for millennia.

I even financed an expedition to Puerto Rico, to search for the fabled Fountain of Youth. It was supposedly known to the Taino Indians before the arrival of the Spanish, in the early sixteenth century. Fruitless, of course.

However if we had not followed every lead, no matter how tenuous, we would not have discovered the miracle of your predecessors."

"But you already said you're not compatible."

"That is why we have dedicated a great deal of resources to investigating you and your counterparts, Mr Allman."

Before I could ask any more questions, the lift doors opened with a chime and dinner arrived. It consisted of venison shanks, served with mixed vegetables, on a bed of garlic mashed potatoes.

I couldn't help but smile, noting that Werewolves aren't affected by garlic.

Topped with a thick gravy, the meal would not have been out of place in a five-star restaurant.

Pearse sat back as the waiter carefully placed the plates in front of us.

He responded with a negative to the question "Will there be anything else, Sir?" and the waiter left.

There was little conversation over the food. Pearse seemed content to enjoy his meal, saving the next chapter of his revelations until we had eaten.

He dabbed his lips with a napkin, and took another sip from his glass.

"Are you sure you won't take a drink, Jack?"

I shook my head. "No, thank you."

"Well then. How about a tour? Hopefully, it will help answer some of your questions."

He pushed back his chair, and gestured towards the lift.

The lift doors opened and I followed him in.

21

Chapter 21

Pearse selected one of the subterranean levels and the doors slid together quietly.

When we exited the lift, it was via the rear.

A corridor extended in front of us. It was lined with windows, giving views into the numerous treatment cubicles on either side.

I recognised some of the pieces of equipment from tests I had undergone in Annie's lab. Others I had never seen before, and could only guess at their function.

Each room had a person, I assumed they were patients, sitting in a chair or on a bed. There were one or two white-coated attendants in each room. They were either talking to their subjects, making observations from the monitors, or connecting the patients to the equipment.

My curiosity was aroused.

"They're all Vukodlak?"

"Homo Lupus, please. But, yes."

"How did you find so many?"

"As a research partner with the Health Service, we have access to medical records. Once we had identified the genetic markers which defined Homo Lupus, we just had to launch a search of the DNA database."

"And then 'persuade' them to join the program."

Pearse looked offended.

"Believe me, Jack, there was no coercion involved. All our subjects are here voluntarily."

"You paid them?"

"Nothing so vulgar. We offered them a cure."

"Cure?"

"All of our volunteers came to us with life-limiting ailments. We are offering the possibility of a reprieve."

I scanned the corridor, trying to estimate the number of 'subjects'.

"And you've turned them all into Werewolves?"

"You just pinpointed the problem, Jack.

No, initially,we treated each of them with synthetic Volsine, initiating the 'shift'."

"Shift?"

"Metamorphosis or transformation are not words which come easily to everyone's tongue. As we are trying to create what were once known as Shapeshifters, one of our laboratory technicians coined the word. Our subjects seem to have taken to it."

"Do they know you're turning them into addicts?"

He looked alarmed.

"Excuse me?"

"The synthetic Volsine. It's addictive and can lead to psychosis."

"No,no. You must be mistaken.There's no mention of that in any of the research. I will need to consult with the project leads. They must be made aware and monitor the patients for any side effects."

He pulled a memostick from his pocket and recorded a brief reminder, before continuing.

"But, as I was saying. The subjects shifted in response to the injection but the lunar transformation failed to materialise."

My importance to Pearse's plan suddenly became apparent.

"I'm the only functioning Lupus you have."

"Very perceptive, Mr Allman. We had hoped to recruit Mr Myers following his escape from captivity but, as Vanguard are already aware, he appears to have gone to ground.

Thankfully, in our investigations, we crossed paths with Agent Walters.

It transpired that he was amenable to persuasion, and that led us to you."

I replayed what I had seen and heard in my head as I tried to make sense of Pearse's plan. It didn't quite add up.

"But, even if you manage to 'activate' them, that still doesn't help you, does it?"

"As you say. But this is only half of the story, Jack. I have another puzzle to solve. Before I can become the Wolf, I must become something else."

"But how? Is it even possible?"

"Don't forget where we are. This is one of the world's premier bio-tech research labs. I have intensive research programs working on stem-cell treatments and genetic manipulation.

You probably know, from your Vanguard colleagues, that I cannot just transplant the infrapituitary gland into my brain, without the corresponding receptors to process the Volsine. I am the opposite of suicidal, Jack. I will do anything it takes to reach my goal."

"I'm sure."

He smiled and shook his head.

"Such cynicism. This has the potential to help hundreds, if not thousands, Jack. It doesn't all begin and end with me.

In the first place, we will be able to activate the gland in Homo Lupus patients and cure them of their ills. Secondly, we want to be able to stimulate growth of receptors in non-Lupus subjects and then treat them as well."

"Yourself included."

He inclined his head, in agreement.

"Dedication to a scientific goal need not necessarily be driven by altruism, Jack."

"So why do you need me?"

"As you rightly point out, you are the only 'functioning' Lupus available. We need to replicate the transmission of the agent which led to Mr Myers' evolution."

"You want me to bite someone?"

He clapped his hands and laughed.

"What a delightful sense of humour you have, Jack. No, I think a saliva sample will suffice, to begin with.

But I am being a poor host. Let me show you to your room. You can rest and consider what you have seen. I will be more than happy to answer any more questions you may have, tomorrow morning."

As prisons go, the room was sumptuous.

There was a living area with floor to ceiling wallscreen and a deep leather sofa. The sleeping area boasted a king-sized bed with auto-drinks makers either side and his and hers sheepskin rugs.

An obscured glass door led through to the ensuite, equipped with jacuzzi bath, surround shower and gold taps on the basin. There was also a small office area, with desk and keyboard, but no telephone.

I pressed a key and the desktop screen flashed to life, displaying a password prompt in the middle.

I wouldn't be sending any messages.

A larder fridge in the living area was stocked with snacks, alcoholic and non-alcoholic drinks and fruit.

I had all the comforts of home but, luxurious or not, I had no intention of staying until morning.

Pearse's welcome had been more cordial than I had expected, and his sales pitch had me intrigued.

If his plans came to fruition, it could certainly revolutionise treatment of serious illness.

There were, to my mind, a few serious flaws. It was unlikely that he'd overlooked them. It was more likely that he'd chosen to ignore them, in his desperate quest to extend his own life.

The most obvious was that each patient, once activated, would be subject to the lunar Pormena. Annie had, thus far, found no way of blocking the release of Volsine. Perhaps Pearse's research was more advanced.

Secondly, the newly-cured would find themselves blessed with a significant strength advantage, compared to the general population. The temptation to abuse that might prove strong for some. They would also enjoy, or suffer, the sharpening of their other senses.

Lastly, I wondered how Pearse would handle the reintegration into society of individuals who might outlive their great-grandchildren.

The more I considered the fallout from his plan, the more I suspected that his great show of philanthropy was nothing more than a screen to justify a single self-centred aim.

I needed to have another tour. Without a chaperone.

I'd tried the door as soon as Pearse left, but wasn't surprised to find it locked.

It was the one utilitarian feature in the room, with three sets of heavy steel hinges, almost impassable, without tools.

Fortunately, I had brought mine with me. Relaxing and concentrating on 'shifting' as Pearse had called it, I soon had a set of obsidian claws, backed by gargantuan muscles to use against the steel clad door.

Inserting a talon into a circular depression at the bottom of the upper hinge, I pushed up against the central pin.

Slowly, at first, but becoming freer as it moved, the pin began to inch its way upwards, until I was able to secure it between two steely claws and pull it out of its seat.

The bottom and middle hinge pins soon followed and ,finally,the door was held in place only by the bolts which had thrown into the frame on the lock side.

I put my ear to the door, relying on my enhanced hearing to warn me if anyone were outside.

Assured that there was no-one in the corridor, I hooked my claws around the hinge side of the door and pulled.

Not designed to endure extreme leverage from this angle, the locking pinions bent and yielded to my attack.

Pulling the door out of the frame, I leaned it against the wall. I looked down the corridor. It was still empty.

There were two doors on the wall opposite and one more on my side, between me and the lift doors.

I listened for movement again, and closed my eyes to read the scent history of the corridor.

While not as acute as when shifted, my sense of smell was keen enough to be certain that there was no-one else in the immediate vicinity. The most recent scents in the corridor were

Pearse's and my own.

It occurred to me that the last time I had been so acutely aware of my own scent was after a particularly strenuous fight scene in a dreadful Space Opera I had filmed the year before.

This was, thankfully, not as unpleasant. In fact, I realised, an occasion might arise where it could be useful to be able to retrace my steps, in the dark.

My room was on the third floor, the same as Pearse's suite.

I should be able to call a lift, without a keycard.

Pressing the button, I waited and watched the indicator, as it climbed from the Ground Floor.

It had crossed my mind to simply escape, flee back to Vanguard and expose Xander for the traitor he was.

However, a better opportunity to determine exactly what Pearse was doing was unlikely to present itself. There was still a faint possibility that I might be wrong about his motives.

Also, I couldn't be sure that others at Vanguard didn't share Xander's opinion. Even Simons didn't seem to be totally un-equivocal as to whether I was an 'asset' or a 'significant risk'. Perhaps throwing my lot in with Pearse might be a better career move.

My anger and disappointment over Xander's betrayal would have to wait.

The muted sound of a bell announced the elevator's arrival, and I braced myself for the possibility of a fight.

The doors parted to reveal the empty interior.

As a general rule, I always assume that someone who locks a room has something to hide, so I was determined to take a look at the lower levels. Without a keycard, I couldn't simply take the lift. I had an alternative strategy.

I leaned into the lift and pressed the button for the fourth floor, pulling back out before the doors closed.

As soon as I could hear the car begin to rise, I forced my claws between the doors and began to pry them apart.

Moments later, I was looking into the lift shaft, as the car stopped on the floor above.

I was in luck. There was a service ladder running down the right hand side wall of the shaft.

Trying not to look down, I swung out across the void, grabbed hold of the ladder, and began to descend as quickly as I could.

The doors on the third floor closed behind me.

I had traversed two floors, when the bell told me that the lift doors had opened again. Someone was getting in on the fourth floor.

I tried to slide down the ladder. I had seen it done dozens of times, in action films. Just put your feet on either side of the ladder and allow it to slide through your hands. But this was real life. I lost my grip and dropped three feet, before arresting my fall, hooking a hand over one of the rungs. I was going to have to do it the old fashioned way, but faster. A lot faster.

As I watched, the counterweights climbed the shaft towards me, and the electrical cables attached to the bottom of the cage began to follow me down the shaft.

I was moving as quickly as I dared, hand over hand down the ladder, but the lift was getting closer.

I doubted that my accelerated healing would save me from a six storey drop.

Then, with barely a sound, the lift came to a halt.

The ground floor. Whoever had called the lift must be leaving the building.

I wiped my forehead with back of my hand, exhaled slowly, and stopped for a moment.

Above me, the lift door closed and it began to move quickly back up the shaft.

I resumed my descent, but had only gone one more floor, when a shadow above alerted me that the lift car was on its way down again.

I was trying to concentrate on making progress down the shaft at maximum speed, without missing a rung on the ladder while keeping an eye on the approaching lift.

It passed the first floor, showing no signs of slowing.

I was in trouble.

It was obvious that I wasn't going to be able to outpace the lift. I stopped and focused my attention on the looming threat, looking for a way to avoid being swept from the ladder.

In the dim light, afforded by the dirty fluorescent tubes lining the shaft, I could just make out a horizontal bar across the bottom of the car.

Waiting until the last possible moment, I relinquished my hold on the ladder and reached for the bar, hoping that my weight would not jar the lift and alert the occupant to my presence.

Before I could congratulate myself on my escape, a new danger presented itself.

The bar was covered in grease, and I was losing my grip.

I looked down and estimated I was still almost three floors from the bottom. I still couldn't see clearly what awaited me below.

The car stopped with a jolt and my left hand slipped from the bar. I was in imminent danger of falling.

I closed my eyes, trying desperately to relax and concentrated on my other hand.

Gradually, I began to feel the familiar warmth in my brain and extended my concentration to unsheath the claws in my right hand.

The steely hooks extended and locked themselves around the bar in a vice-like grip.

With a secure hold, I was now able to reach up and do the same with my left hand.

I hung there, breathing heavily.

The lift doors closed above me and the car resumed its descent.

As it neared the bottom, I could make out the spring-loaded buffers in the space below.

I released my grip and dropped lightly to the dusty concrete floor, crouching in the darkness as the lift came to a halt above me.

I squatted, waiting, in the void. Finally, I could relax.

At least ten minutes must have passed, before the lift started its journey back up the shaft, but I was in no hurry.

Standing, I brushed myself off and turned my attention to the doors, which were at waist height.

I cracked them open and peered down a short corridor. It was empty.

Forcing the doors open wide enough to get my shoulders through, I pulled myself up and on to the carpet.

I stopped, listened, and sampled the air. Pearse was down here.

Behind me, the lift closed quietly.

There were three doors off the corridor, one either side, one at the end.

Pearse's scent trail ran, straight as an arrow, to the door in front of me.

22

Chapter 22

I approached the door, listening for any hint of activity on the other side.

Hearing nothing, I tried the handle.

It turned easily, and I opened the door and stepped through, closing it quietly behind me.

I found myself in a dimly lit corridor which opened into a larger space beyond.

Once inside, I could hear movement ahead. Hugging the wall, I crept forward.

The room was immense. The centre was in near darkness but I could make out what appeared to be a circular cage around ten feet tall and twenty feet across. As far as I could make out, it was empty. I closed my eyes. To my scent radar, it lit up like a bonfire. I tried to make sense of the overpowering mixture of odours emanating from its floor.

Human, Wolf, bleach, sweat, unidentifiable chemicals. Blood?

Up ahead, in a pool of light, Pearse sat with his back to me, at a large conference table. He was alone.

The last third of the corridor was lined on both sides with booths which resembled the treatment rooms I had seen on the higher floor but these were currently unoccupied.

I slid into the nearest cubicle and ducked behind a cabinet.

The level of illumination in the room was growing.

Peering over the top of the cabinet, I could see floating luminous nuclei expanding in the air above the table. Pearse was hosting a conference via holo-presence.

He busied himself at a keypad. One by one, the holo-solids sharpened as each attendee connected.

With every space around the table filled, he greeted his guests.

"A very good evening Ladies and Gentlemen. And a good day to those of you in other time zones.

I have excellent progress to report.

Firstly, I have secured the vector which will permit us to achieve a full conversion.

Secondly, we have commenced a final human trial on the lupogenesis treatment."

A woman with asian features interrupted him. She spoke with an English accent.

"When do you anticipate you will be able to combine the two and achieve end-to-end enhancement?"

"That depends on the outcome of this trial Ms Park but, as you will see, it appears to be proceeding smoothly."

He touched the keypad and a new holo-solid formed above the table.

It showed one of the cubicles in the treatment area. The occupant was sitting up in bed, connected to an an intravenous infusion. Although there was no sound, it was obvious that he was arguing with one of his attendants and appeared to be in restraints.

Pearse continued.

"He was another unfortunate we found sleeping rough. For

a city which was built to represent a new start, there are many inhabitants who appear to have no hope for their future. This one has no concept of the gift with which we are about to endow him."

He and his guests studied the patient intently, and I did the same.

There was something familiar about his face. They had shaved his head to apply electrodes and trimmed his beard to blonde stubble but there was no mistaking the his identity. Daisy.

My heart sank. There was no way I could even attempt a rescue. My priority had to be to collect as much information as possible and escape, back to Vanguard. I could only hope that Daisy could hold out until I was able to return with reinforcements.

Any hope I'd harboured that Pearse had been telling me the whole truth evaporated. Now I knew what had been happening to the missing homeless. They were unwilling subjects in Pearse's experiments.

A white-haired man, picked up the conversation.

"Und, if it fails?"

"All the indications are that that is a highly unlikely outcome, Herr Junker. However, we are always mindful of the possibility of failure. Therefore, you will be pleased to know that we are very close to an alternative solution with the Sangroid Project." responded Pearse, reassuringly.

The holo-image pursed its lips, and nodded.

"So, my esteemed colleagues, you will shortly be seeing a return on your investments. Longevity is within our grasp."

"There is still no way to prevent the Lunar shift?"

The question came from a thick-set woman who sounded Eastern European. She appeared to be in her sixties.

Pearse scowled at the interruption.

"As I have said before, Marta, that is hardly a priority. Spending one night a month in a magnificent Wolf body is a small sacrifice for the wealth and influence you will achieve, given an additional hundred years to manage your affairs."

"I would rather avoid spending a single second as a filthy dog, if it can be prevented." she complained.

"Well, given another century to continue my research, who knows what might be possible." Pearse smiled, thinly.

"If there is no other business, I think it's high time for this week's entertainment. To those of you not remaining to enjoy our spectacle, I wish you adieu until our next update."

Several of the holo-solids faded to transparency, before blinking out completely. It appeared that the majority of those who remained were men, except for the Eastern European woman whose face had come alive with anticipation.

Pearse's fingers played over the keypad and, suddenly the room was flooded with light.

I ducked behind the cabinet hoping I wouldn't be detected.

There was a sound of sliding doors opening and I risked a glance around the side of the drawers to get a better look through the glass partition wall.

The circular cage which dominated the middle of the room had a door at the back, which was now open.

Behind it were two openings in the wall, which I hadn't seen in the dark.

From each one came an orderly, leading someone dressed in a hospital gown.

As they emerged into the light, I realised they were both women. I had seen one of them, earlier, in the treatment area.

She would be in her late teens, a heavy girl with close-cropped black hair and a tattoo of a climbing rose snaking up her left arm. She looked confident, arrogant even. She stared at the other woman with disdain.

The other was older, probably in her forties. She appeared to have a nervous twitch, shaking her head to clear her lank mousy hair from her face. She scratched at her forearms constantly. Her eyes flicked continuously from side to side. Slightly built, her physique was more athletic but verging on anorexic.

Both women were ushered into the cage and the door closed behind them.

They moved to opposite sides of the enclosure and each extended an arm through a gap in the bars where their individual attendants waited.

The tension around the table was palpable, the watchers leaning forward for a better view.

I could have sworn the woman was almost salivating and a wave of nausea hit me as I understood what was about to happen.

Pearse stepped away from the table and positioned himself between the cage and the audience.

"Honoured guests, welcome to tonight's event. Assuming that you have all completed your wagers, I present our combatants."

He pointed first to the older woman.

"Victorious in seven encounters, and our longest-serving volunteer, Diana."

He addressed her directly.

"A double dose of happiness if you succeed tonight, my Goddess of the hunt. Yes?"

Her darting eyes fixed on him and she nodded her head, grinning wildly.

Sadly, I realised that she must be a serial synthetic Volsine user. She looked to be totally insane. Pearse's feigned shock, when I'd told him of the side effects, was obviously all part of his act.

He turned back to his viewers.

"Her opponent is a new addition to our program. She has tasted the delights of our synthetic Volsine and fights tonight for her next indulgence. I give you Asha."

The dark-haired girl raised her arms over her head, her fists clenched.

Pearse ended his introduction with a single word.

"Begin."

The attendants produced transdermal hyposprays and applied them to the women's forearms.

Having administered the drugs, their part in the horror which was about to unfold was done. They exited through the sliding doors, which closed behind them.

As the combatants began to shift, it occurred to me that I couldn't sense either of them. There was no connection, not even a hint of empathy. Perhaps it only came after the infection, Pearse's 'vector', had activated the infrapituitary.

The dark-haired girl's face was a picture of ecstasy and I felt a twinge of envy, knowing how she was feeling, quickly erased by the memory of the synthetic hormone's withdrawal effects.

She watched, smiling, as her arms began to swell, splitting the hospital gown.

The older woman, a veteran of the cage, was not so easily distracted.

Before she had even finished shifting, she raced across the cage towards her opponent. Throwing herself to the floor, she slid, feet-first across the mat. As she passed the still-shifting girl, she lashed out with her emerging claws, severing the tendon at the back of her adversary's left heel.

Howling with pain, the younger woman scythed wildly at the floor behind her but her attacker was gone.

Recovering her feet, the now fully transformed light-pelted wolf jumped, landing high up the back of her limping victim. She reached around her opponent's head and tore savagely at her face.

Engaged, the black wolf sank her claws into her attacker's arms and pulled her completely over her head throwing her across the cage. The older Wolf hit the bars with a bone-shaking impact.

The bigger, younger combatant followed her across the mat. She was limping heavily and, from the way she held her head off-centre, having difficulty seeing with her right eye. Blood matted the fur across her cheek.

Her opponent lay curled on the floor where she fell. She had not moved since the impact and the bigger wolf stood over her with both arms raised and claws ready to strike.

She paused, tipped her head back and roared to announce her impending victory.

In the blink of an eye her intended victim uncoiled like a spring and rolled to the wall of the cage. Using her claws as a mountaineer uses ice hooks she swiftly scaled the wall. Reaching the roof she hung, upside down, using all four sets of talons to hold her position.

The younger Wolf was the taller of the two but even with her height advantage, she was unable to reach her adversary. She tried to jump but, hampered by her injured heel, she landed badly and stumbled. Before she could recover her balance, the other traversed the ceiling of the cage and released her grip, to drop behind her. Leaping on her back again, to avoid the black wolf's powerful arms, the veteran fighter began tearing at her victim's head and neck, almost severing one of her ears.

Even without an empathetic link, I could smell the younger wolf's fear.

She staggered backwards again but, instead of trying to correct her imbalance, she jumped as high as she could. Hampered by a shredded ankle and the weight of her opponent, the height of the jump was limited but she angled her body so that her full mass came down on top of her attacker.

As they landed, there was a sickening crunch and the smaller wolf yelped in pain.

Before she could extricate herself, the black wolf spun around and raked her front claws viciously across her helpless opponent's belly.

Again the lighter Wolf's speed saved her and she squirmed and backed away from her attacker.

They both dropped to all fours and circled each other anti-clockwise around the cage. Both looking for an opportunity to launch another attack. The older Wolf was bleeding heavily from her abdominal wound. They growled at each other, waving razor-sharp claws threateningly.

Without warning, the lighter Wolf switched direction and began to circle in a clockwise direction. Her younger adversary followed suit. Too late she realised that it had been a tactic to force her to turn her injured eye to her opponent.

The attack was swift and ferocious. Although smaller, the light Wolf hit the larger with enough force to throw her on her side. She gripped her throat between her front paws and began tearing at her belly with the talons on her hind legs.

The younger yelped, but brought up her own back legs to block the assault, and reached for her attacker with her front claws.

The grey wolf snapped at the grasping hand, trying to catch it between her jaws, but the black talons found their target and closed around her windpipe. Moments later, the black Wolf had both sets of claws tightly locked on to her victim's throat.

Pinned, the older wolf flailed wildly, trying to claw her opponent's already ravaged face.

It was no use. Her attacker had the advantage of a much longer reach and, as I watched, her resistance became weaker and weaker.

Having been fooled once, the younger Wolf was taking no chances and maintained her grip long after her adversary was still.

Finally, she struggled to an upright stance, still clutching the lifeless body of the other beast.

Clamping her massive jaws around its throat, she began to tear at the corpse until the head separated from the body.

Allowing the carcase to fall to the floor, she held her trophy aloft and shook the room with a blood-curdling howl of victory.

It was met with cheers from the remaining members of Pearse's holo-conference.

My reaction to the scent of gore was more of fascination than revulsion but my still-human sensibilities revolted against the exploitation of Pearse's 'volunteers' for the entertainment of his colleagues.

Now I knew the reality of his research and the depth of his moral depravity. I vowed that I would sooner go down fighting than allow myself to be used to promote his agenda.

Granting the members of his twisted club an extra hundred years of life to fulfil their selfish plans did not figure in any plan of mine.

The attendants reappeared and the battered victor was helped, limping, from the ring. The remains of the loser, for now, were left where they had fallen.

I wondered what sort of state the black wolf would be in, once the Pormena ended. Pearse had already indicated that 'inactivated' Vukodlak did not share my regenerative powers.

The audience were exchanging farewells with their host. The scowling woman did not look happy. I suspected that the fight had not lasted long enough to satisfy her bloodlust. I surpressed a smirk at the idea that such an evil bitch should balk at the thought of spending time as a dog.

The remaining holo-solids blinked off and Pearse turned out the lights over his arena.

For a few minutes more, he busied himself at the keypad then, killing the remaining lights over the table, he turned and headed for the lift.

I shrank back against the wall and held my breath as he passed my cubicle.

It occurred to me that, if he could see my scent as I could see his, he would already have discovered my presence. As it was, he passed me by without a backward glance.

I waited until I heard the lift doors close behind him before I emerged from cover.

There was little of interest in the room. The cubicles were all virtually identical and showed no signs of recent use.

In the semi darkness, the scent of the body in the cage shone like a beacon. At the moment, her remains were still those of a wolf. I wondered if they would return to human.

I now knew the truth behind Pearse's plan. I recalled Volkov's final words 'no more Vukodlak'. I had already failed to honour his last wish, when I unwittingly infected Dylan Myers. I promised myself it would not happen again. I would not be responsible for extending the lives of the mega-rich and bringing the Vukodlak back into the world.

Right now, my priority was to return to Vanguard. Simons had to know about Pearse. And Xander's betrayal.

Pearse had already taken the lift. I didn't dare call it. If he saw it descending to the underground meeting room, he might become suspicious.

When I prised open the outer doors of the lift shaft, the cage was already out of sight above me. I swung across to the ladder, and began my ascent.

I reached the level of the underground car park without incident. I imagine that most office-hours staff had gone home and Pearse had returned to his sanctum.

I forced the doors apart and scanned the parking area. There didn't appear to be any security cameras. My only other option for leaving was a brazen stroll through reception, as if I were a worker leaving for the night. I didn't fancy my chances. If there were reception or security staff, I was bound to be challenged.

Exiting the shaft, I strolled casually up the ramp. If I was being observed, I didn't want to look suspicious.

At the top of the slope there was no barrier, but a steel roller door blocked my path.

I shifted my arms, engaged my claws and began to force it open.

The lights in the car park changed to flashing red and my acute hearing was assailed by a squawking klaxon.

I'd triggered an alarm.

Redoubling my efforts, I lifted the door to waist height and ducked under, out into the cool of the night.

Cool it might have been, but not dark. High intensity spot-lights flooded the area around the building. I had no choice but to make a run for it.

Taking a deep breath, I concentrated on directing Volsine to my legs. This was a time for escaping, not fighting.

As I sprinted across the concrete apron between the building and the surrounding fence, I could hear shouts behind me.

A moment later, the voices were drowned out by shots, as bullets ricocheted around me. I zigzagged, hoping that my Vukodlak-enhanced speed would evade the aim of the shooters.

I almost stumbled as my shift caused me to lose my shoes but recovered in time to tense myself for a huge leap at the perimeter fence.

Surprising myself,I cleared it easily. Beyond the glare of the lights, I continued running.

I had only a vague idea of where I was, in the industrial district, but had to put Novo Lupus as far behind me as possible.

The shooting had stopped. They were not wasting bullets firing blind but the buildings in front of me lit up in the head-lights of pursuing cars. I doubted I could outrun them, even fully shifted.

I turned in to an alley, to be suddenly dazzled by a vehicle's headlights, pointing straight at me.

I stopped, and prepared myself to fight but in the moments it took to shift from legs back to arms, the lights dimmed and a voice called from the darkness beyond.

"Jack, over here."

It was agent Mochales, the weapons instructor.

I ran, barefoot, towards the car.

Diego held the door open, staring wide-eyed at my arms. The

claws were retracting and the black hairs were receding under the skin, as my biceps and forearms returned to their normal size.

"Neat trick, mate." He mused "Get in."

"What are you doing here, Diego?!"

"The Boss has had one of us on standby, ever since you went in."

"You knew I was in there but never thought to come in and get me?"

He smiled again "Orders are orders, Jack."

We drove the rest of the way to Vanguard in silence.

I was saving my revelations for Simons.

23

Chapter 23

From the car park, we headed straight for Simons' office.

Xander was there, with his back to the door.

He turned, an expression of surprise on his face.

Then he smiled "Welcome back, Bud…"

His sentence went unfinished as my fist caught him full in the face and threw him backwards against the far wall. My anger fuelled my Wolf-enhanced muscles.

Before he could regain his feet, I lunged forward, to press my advantage.

Diego grabbed my arm, in a futile attempt to restrain me. Simons stepped between us.

"Jack. Enough."

"But he … you don't know…" In my fury, I was almost incoherent.

"That he handed you over to Pearse? He did it on my instructions."

What?

I shook my head, confused.

"Why would you?"

"We needed intelligence. Agent Walters' informant had put

Pearse in touch with Xander. It took some time, but he was able to present himself as a credible double-agent.

An agreement was reached, and a price set for your delivery.

Neither Walters nor I were particularly keen on putting you in harm's way, and we were working on a plan of support, and extrication, if necessary.

Then Doctor Dixon brought me the news of your revelation. It rather put a different perspective on things. I took the chance that you could look after yourself, and sent you in."

Xander was still sitting on the floor, wiping his bloody nose with a handkerchief.

"Xander. I'm sorry. I didn't know."

He grinned from behind the blood-soaked cloth.

"No, Buddy. I'm sorry you were dropped in at the deep end. From what our observers tell us, you stirred up quite a hornets' nest. Good right, by the way."

I held out the offending hand and helped him to his feet.

"That was quite an act, in the warehouse. Are you, by any chance, after my old job?"

"Yeah, well. Forget what I said. It was just to make you more receptive to Pearse's invitation, and a little show to stop him getting suspicious."

"Wait. You knew that I could manage a partial shift?"

His sheepish expression was all the answer I needed.

"That's why you made the comment about about having Jackalman with you. I thought that was odd, at the time."

"Yeah. I nearly let the cat out of the bag. Or the Wolf, at any rate."

I shook his hand and clapped him on the shoulder with the other.

His apparent betrayal had unbalanced me more than I had

cared to admit.

Some of the things he had said had hit a little too close to home. While it was a relief to have my faith restored, I still had to accept that some of the points he had made might be valid.

Simons interrupted the moment.

"Now we're all friends again, perhaps Mr Allman can share what he learnt.

Diego, would you ask Doctor Dixon to join us."

Annie almost ran down the corridor, burst into the office and threw her arms around my neck. She held me for longer than I was expecting.

"Jack. You're alright! I was so worried."

Over her shoulder, Simons' face was a picture of consternation. Xander tried to suppress a smile at my obvious embarrassment.

As I half-heartedly returned the greeting, Annie seemed to suddenly realise that we were not alone in the office and abruptly disengaged. A secret smile on her face said 'later' and she resumed her professional demeanour.

I was pleased to see her too. Xander's little speech at the warehouse had given me pause for thought. We had grown closer over the previous weeks, but was there any future in it?

If I'd learnt one thing since my brush with death, it was that I was done letting Fate make my decisions for me. I'd had my parents snatched away before their time. My Predak, Hedoen Volokov had been eliminated before I'd had a chance to get to know him.

I'd been a lone Wolf long enough.

"Are we quite done?" asked Simons, curtly. "Mr Allman, the room is yours."

I started my story from the point where Xander had left me with Pearse and his goons.

No-one said a word until I began to describe the underground treatment bays.

"Could you tell how many subjects he had, overall?" asked Simons.

"Only about a dozen at present but his principal aim is not to produce an army of weaponised Vukodlak, as Volkov feared."

He looked perplexed. "What then?"

"He wants to turn non-Vukodlak into what he terms Homo Lupus. Himself included."

"But why would he....?"

It was Annie who answered.

"A life expectancy of two hundred years or more."

"And he's not alone." I continued "He has a dozen or so backers, all chasing the same prize. I saw a lot of them in holoconference. This is an international enterprise."

Xander whistled. "A gang of corporate fat cats, with lifespans over three times that of normal humans. You can accumulate a lot of wealth and gain a lot of influence in three lifetimes."

Simons' face was serious.

"Continue, please, Mr Allman."

I described the medical bays I had seen and recounted how Pearse had recruited his volunteers, with the promise of a Panacea. A cure for all their ills, provided they were Homo Lupus.

I described how he was deliberately getting them hooked on synthetic Volsine, to the extent that they would fight to the death for their next fix.

Simons' expression hardened and Annie hid her face in her hands.

She was both fascinated and horrified by Pearse's experiments to create Homo Lupus with genetic modification and stem cell therapy.

While neither Xander nor Simons knew Daisy, both agreed that Pearse was probably behind the spate of homeless disappearances.

When I finished my sorry tale, it was Simons who broke the silence.

"Thank you, Mr Allman. And well done on your first foray into the field."

I was still irked by the fact that I had been thrown in the deep end, and allowed to believe that Xander had betrayed me, but accepted the compliment.

"Thanks, but that was quite a risk you took, sending me in. If Pearse had got his hands on a sample of my saliva, we could be looking at a pack of new werewolves. They would have inherited my regenerative abilities too, unlike the poor sods Pearse has fighting in his cage."

"Quite so, Mr Allman. Although,both I and Agent Walters had every confidence that your moral compass would guide you back to Vanguard. Be that as it may, Ambrose Pearse is now our top priority. We have to terminate his operation, before he has a chance to bring his plan to fruition."

"And before he can harm any more innocent people."

Annie said what I was thinking, before I could get the words out. She shifted her gaze from Simons to me, and we shared a conspiratorial smile.

Simons grunted and stood up behind his desk.

"Yes, well. Perhaps you would lead the way to your laboratory, Doctor Dixon, and show us what you have been working on."

We followed her out of the office.

Annie stood before her display screen, like a teacher in front of class.

Simons stood alongside her, and gave his preamble.

"Since we discovered that Volkov was working to end a plot to reintroduce the Vukodlak, or Homo Lupus if you prefer, we have had to consider what defensive measures we might need to take, if faced with such a formidable foe.

Our initial misgivings about weaponised Wolves have, thankfully, proved to be groundless. However, Pearse has shown that he is quite willing to drive his volunteers to dependence on synthetic Volsine for entertainment. It's quite possible that he would also use them for defence. With that in mind, I charged various Departments, including Medical, with formulating countermeasures.

If you please. Doctor."

With a wave of her hand, Annie woke her screen. It displayed what looked like a diagram of some chemical compound.

"This," she began "is the molecular structure of synthetic Volsine. While this " she waved her hand in front of the screen and it flashed momentarily "is a new compound I have created by reverse engineering the original. "

Xander beat me to the punch by asking "There's a difference?"

Annie rolled her eyes and waved her hand in front of the screen again, flicking from one image to the other and back again.

This time I was able to see the difference, albeit small, between the two diagrams.

"Yes, we see, Doctor" interrupted Simons "but would you be so kind as to explain the significance of your work?"

"Well, based on the research notes recovered from the murdered scientists, it would appear that Volsine, both natural and synthetic, is metabolised very quickly by the body.

183

This means that its effects are short-lived. A constant output of natural Volsine, or a very high dose of the synthetic variant, is required to maintain Pormena for any length of time.

What I have created is a neutered form of synthetic Volsine."

"Neutered?" scowled Simons.

"It imitates Volsine and locks into the receptors, but doesn't activate transformation. Plus, it metabolises much slower than Volsine.

By the time the receptors are free to accept Volsine again, at least in the case of the synthetic variant, there is none left as the body has already removed it from the bloodstream."

"So this could prevent Pormena?" Xander offered.

"Better still. It could reverse an existing transformation." Annie smiled and blanked her screen.

Simons clapped his hands "Very impressive, Doctor. Was there something else?"

Annie frowned. "Well, I provided some clinical information to weapons R&D, based on the physiological tests I did with Jack in his Wolf form.

They came up with a prototype device. It's rather unsophisticated and will require tuning in the field but I believe it could give us an advantage in a fight."

She unlocked a small cart and opened the lid. The weapon she took out resembled a steampunk version of an eighteenth-century blunderbuss.

A stock like a shotgun connected to a thick body, sprouting knobs, dials and variable slider controls. The whole assembly terminated in a flared cone, like a trumpet.

Xander began to laugh, but his amusement withered under Simons' baleful gaze.

Annie looked sheepish "Yes, I know it might look like something from one of Jack's Space Operas, but I'm assured it packs a punch."

"How does it work?" Xander had recovered his composure.

"Normal human hearing has an upper frequency limit of 23,000 hertz. Canine hearing can typically register sounds up to 45,000 hertz. In the higher ranges, dogs will find these sounds uncomfortable.

This device emits a directional blast in excess of 40,000 hertz. It should be enough to disorientate a Wolf, but its field of projection is quite narrow, so it's only going to be effective on one opponent at once.

I would envisage it being used in parallel with the Volsine blocker."

"Zap 'em then dart 'em." quipped Xander.

"Yes, very succinct, Agent Walters. You say there is only one of these devices, Doctor?" asked Simons.

"Unfortunately, yes. However, I've managed to fabricate enough of the Volsine blocker to fill several dozen hypo darts."

"And if all else fails, we have Plan B." smiled Xander, grimly.

I didn't like the sound of that.

"What do you mean?"

"Silver bullets, Nube. And, if those don't stop a raging Wolf, we have some nifty gas grenades that release a cloud of aerosolised silver particles. That should make the buggers cough."

"Yes, and me too. Thanks." I was outraged. "Let's not forget that, apart from being hooked on synthetic Volsine, these potential opponents are victims. They were inducted into Pearse's program under false pretences, with a promise of a potential cure. You're talking about killing sick people."

"OK, OK. No gas grenades, Jeesus."

"Anyhow," I added "you can't be sure that silver will affect them. I didn't develop the allergy until after I was bitten."

"A bullet is still a bullet, Buddy." he smiled in reply.

"On this occasion, I have to agree with Mr Allman." nodded Simons. "Non-lethal force only."

I remembered what Volkov had told me about the effects of Volsine on non-Vukodlak and asked if the Volsine blocker could be harmful to humans. I was getting used to considering the Human Race to be a club of which I was no longer a member.

"It shouldn't be a problem." Annie reassured the group. "As the blocker isn't engineered to induce any changes, just to block the receptors, there should be no ill effects on humans."

"Shouldn't be. Great" muttered Xander "I'd still feel safer with a silver grenade on my belt."

He, Diego and Simons left, to coordinate preparations for a strike on Novo Lupus, leaving me alone with Annie.

24

Chapter 24

As soon as everyone had left the room, Annie rushed to me and threw her arms around my neck.

"Jack. I didn't realise they were going to send you out straight away. By the time I got back to my office, you were gone.

Simons told me not to worry, but I had an awful feeling that I might not see you again.

That was when I realised."

"Realised?"

"Don't be so dim, Jack." She pulled my head down towards her, and kissed me.

The heat rising in my face was the same feeling I had had when I was injected with the synthetic hormone. A rush of elation. I pulled her closer and returned the kiss.

"Mr Allman, " she laughed, "there is life in the old dog."

I said nothing. I couldn't tear my gaze away from her incredibly blue eyes.

"Say something, Jack."

"Sorry. It's been a difficult couple of days. After what Xander said to me, in the warehouse, I was having my doubts."

"About?"

"This...us. Whether it could be." I turned away. "I'm not even human any more, Annie."

She grabbed my arm and spun me back around to face her.

"You are human, and more. You're kind, funny, honest and intelligent. I can relax with you, in a way that I can't with other people.

What you are isn't as important as who you are.

Fyi, I'm not perfect either.

I'll admit, I've had my doubts about my feelings. It's all too easy for a physician to become emotionally invested in a patient.

I thought we'd lost you, the week after the attack."

"But you didn't. You saved my life. How can I be sure that what I'm feeling isn't just some sort of exaggerated gratitude?"

"What if I told you I almost killed you?"

"What?"

"When you first came in, the surgeons treated your wounds and patched you up. Then they handed you over to Medical, to oversee your recovery.

Things didn't go well."

"Simons told me. You tried all sorts of drugs and antibiotics."

"I did, and your condition worsened.

Blood work showed an unknown infection. We treated it as sepsis. We threw everything at it, antibiotics, antivirals. The more we gave you, the more your condition deteriorated. The infection resisted all our drugs.

In the end, there was nothing else we could do. We ceased all infusions, moved you to a quiet room, and waited for the inevitable outcome."

There were tears in her eyes. I reached out and pulled her closer.

"But I got it wrong. Within twenty-four hours, your condition had improved.

Forty-eight hours after we withdrew treatment, your vital signs had stabilised, your temperature had dropped.

Two days later, you woke up."

"And I felt great."

"But the infection was still present. That's why I had Xander keep an eye on you, when you went home. You were perfectly fit, but still infected.

I had no way of knowing, at the time, what was going to happen next."

"But is it still there?"

"Yes, Jack. The infection is what saved you."

"I don't understand."

"The infection is what makes you Vukodlak. It activates the receptors, allows the Volsine to be metabolised. It's responsible for your regenerative abilities.

While I was saturating your System with antibiotics, I was suppressing its effects. As soon as I stopped drug therapy, it was able to multiply, spread and do its work.

It wasn't the infection which kept you in a coma for so long, it was my treatment.

I'm so sorry."

She pressed her face to my chest.

I stroked her hair.

"Don't beat yourself up about it. At least one of us is only human."

She wriggled out of my grasp and began to pound on my chest with her fists.

"You!" she gasped, half crying, half laughing.

I caught her wrists and pulled her in again.

"So, Doctor. Any other confessions?"

189

She stopped laughing and tipped her head back, to look me in the face, suddenly serious.

"Jack. I know you've been feeling like an outsider, some sort of alien.

I have something to tell you which might put things into perspective."

She bowed her head, and I waited. When she looked up again, she said,

"I'm a mermaid."

For a moment, I was speechless. I spluttered.

"But...how? I...when? No. Seriously?"

"No, you dope. I'm the Queen of the Fairies.

Really, Jack. Would it make any difference?"

"Of course not."

"My point exactly. So shut up and kiss me again.

Then we've got work to do."

25

Chapter 25

My escape from Novo Lupus had not been the stealthy exit I had envisioned. Pearse would be expecting a visit from Vanguard.

There was little time to formulate a plan. We would have to strike quickly, before he had time to evacuate his patients and staff.

Simons had called a Pre-op briefing with TAC squad leaders. Xander had organised distribution of the blocker darts to drone sniper operators and agents who would be on the ground. That included me.

Simons informed me that Diego had certified me Weapons Ready. I was issued with a sidearm, albeit with a non-lethal payload.

By 3 a.m. we were ready to roll.

A caravan of lightly armoured vehicles snaked out of the Vanguard compound and rumbled through the night towards Novo Lupus.

We all wore bullet-proof vests and vgoggles with night-vision enhancement and target assistance HUD.

Annie sat next to me, cocooned in an over-large vest, cradling her sonic weapon in her lap.

I felt uneasy about her taking part but she insisted. "I'm the only one who can make on-the-fly adjustments to the output spectrum and troubleshoot any last minute problems."

It was true. The weapon's designers in their underground labs would soil themselves at the mere suggestion of taking their prototype into the field personally.

Within twenty-five minutes, Vanguard operatives ringed the Novo Lupus building, with sniper drone operators on adjoining roofs and patrols in the surrounding streets. Streets which were blocked by Vanguard vehicles.

At a signal from Simons, the first TAC squad approached the front of the building.

The moment their boots touched the concrete apron, high-intensity floodlights illuminated the area around the structure. They paused and squatted, scanning the building for movement, allowing their vgoggles to adjust to the increased light intensity.

I half expected gunfire but, when there was none, the Squad Leader motioned his men forward, approaching the entrance in a half-crouch.

Suddenly there was a noise.

They were still advancing. They hadn't heard it. I turned my head, trying to focus on the source.

The roller door on the car park ramp. I alerted Simons.

"We have company. Coming from the left side of the building. I can't see anything yet, but I can hear them ."

Without hesitating to query my warning, Simons passed it to the Squad Leader and he turned his contingent to face the threat.

The shutter began to rise.

Silhouetted in the light from further down the ramp, I could make out around a dozen figures. There were men and women, all dressed in tracksuits. They did not appear to be carrying weapons. One of them stepped forward. It was Pearse.

"Supervisory Agent Simons." he shouted, addressing himself to the darkness beyond the perimeter, "this is a lawfully registered medical facility. My patients are here voluntarily. I invite you and your soldiery to leave our property and avoid an unpleasant incident."

Simons' reply was distorted by a loud-hailer "We respectfully decline your invitation, Mr Pearse. We will be entering your premises, collecting evidence and detaining certain individuals for interview, to support our enquiries."

"As you wish." he turned to his companions "Ladies and gentlemen. The time has come to defend our research."

Each of the tracksuited individuals produced a transdermal hypospray from their pockets and pressed it to the side of their neck. Within seconds their expressions changed to ecstasy as the synthetic Volsine took effect.

As I watched, each one of them began to shift. Within less than a minute, we were faced with over a dozen Werewolves of different sizes and colours.

As if on a signal, the pack burst and the Wolves ran in different directions, some towards the squad near the entrance and some towards the other Vanguard Agents waiting, just beyond the illuminated apron.

Pearse stood, watching from the top of the ramp.

The firing started, but the Wolves were fast and hard to hit in the darkness. There were screams as they found their targets. They had no need of night-vision goggles, they could hunt by scent alone.

Annie was trying to aim her unwieldy weapon. With an approaching Wolf in her sights, she stabbed at the activator button. All I could hear was a faint whistle, but the Wolf stopped, as if it had been slapped across the muzzle. Its momentary hesitation was long enough for a Vanguard agent to take a shot with his dart gun. The projectile embedded itself in the Wolf's thigh. It looked down and plucked the dart from its flesh, dropping it on the concrete.

Tipping back its head and howling, it strode towards the Agent, arms raised and claws ready to attack. But, before it could strike, it stopped.

It held up its paws, confused. The claws had retracted. It shook its arm, as if that would extend the vicious talons, but to no avail. It lurched forward and stumbled. Its legs appeared to be shrinking. Its whole bulk was diminishing. It realised too late that its Pormena was over.

Before the now fully human opponent could turn to run, the Vanguard Agent was on him, handcuffs ready.

Annie was selecting her next target, and I readied my dart pistol.

Suddenly I stopped. The sounds of combat around me seemed to fade into the distance.

There was someone in my head. A familiar presence. Dylan Myers! What was he doing here?

I spun around, trying to locate him in the surrounding melee. Agents were running in all directions, trying to stay out of reach of the razor-sharp Wolves' claws. Others were overpowering the Homo Lupus who had been hit with the neutralising darts.

I tried to block out the shouting, shooting, roaring and screaming and pinpoint Dylan's location. Closing my eyes, I inhaled deeply, seeking his scent.

I had him. He was behind me. Turning back, I saw the giant red Wolf, bearing down on Annie.

A Vanguard Agent shoved her out of the way, only to fall victim to Dylan's scything attack.

I ran directly towards them. Annie was struggling to regain her feet, looking around her for the sonic weapon. She had dropped it, when the Agent had pushed her out of harm's way. It lay on the ground beside her, bent and useless. Dylan threw the Agent's lifeless body out into the darkness and turned his attention back to Annie.

I projected a thought, with all the strength I could muster

"Dylan. Over here."

He stopped in mid-stride. Tilting his huge head to one side, he sniffed the air, searching. He turned. He recognised me. I could hear him laughing, inside my head.

"Got you now, man. Let's see who gets bitten this time."

I raised my pistol, took careful aim, and fired. He swatted the dart, as if it were a fly.

"Seriously, Dude?"

He spun to his left and hooked his claws into Annie's vest, lifting her off the ground.

"No!" Whether I said it aloud, or in my head, Dylan recognised my desperation.

Dangling her in front of me, he laughed aloud.

"Come and get her, Hero." echoed in my brain.

There was another voice, not in my head, but in my earpiece. It was Simons.

"Agent Allman. Deploy Anubis. I repeat. Deploy Anubis. That's an order, Jack."

I dropped my weapon and allowed my arms to fall to my sides. Myers chuckled, apparently interpreting my actions as capitulation.

I exhaled slowly and closed my eyes. Clenching my fists, I focused on the infrapituitary.

I tried to block from my mind the vision of the red-pelted giant holding Annie aloft. I had to concentrate. If I couldn't evoke the Pormena, Annie and I were as good as dead.

I visualised the gland, producing Volsine. I began to feel the warmth, spreading into my neck, down into my chest. But it was happening too slowly.

Then Annie screamed. She wasn't a screamer. It wasn't a reaction to fear. Dylan's claws were puncturing her vest and finding flesh.

Still in human form, I howled with rage and the infrapituitary went into overdrive. The flood of hormone hitting my brain was almost akin to my first synthetic Volsine experience. The shift was so rapid it almost threw me off balance.

I could feel the disbelief in Dylan's mind.

"How? It's not a full moon."

Resisting the overwhelming urge to howl, I pressed home the advantage of surprise and threw myself at the red Wolf, hitting it square in the chest. As it fell on to its back, its claws opened and Annie rolled free.

I had no time to check on her, I had to try and finish Dylan, while he was down.

Swinging wildly, I opened gouges across his chest, as he roared with pain.

His back legs came up and kicked me in the belly, throwing me six feet across the concrete. He lurched to his feet and came at me. I was severely mismatched. As a human, Dylan had been taller than me. As a Wolf, he was a formidable creature.

I assumed he was also the more experienced fighter. We stood, toe to toe, trading blows. His claws raked across my face, narrowly missing my left eye. I made a fist and swung at his muzzle. He dodged easily. This wasn't a fist fight. I had to fight like an animal and use the weapons at hand.

I recalled the tactic one of the cage fighting women had used at Novo Lupus. It was worth a try, and I was desperate.

I managed to step back a couple of paces, to give myself room to manoeuvre. Throwing myself towards my opponent, I dropped to the floor and slid under his swinging attack, reaching out to slice at him in passing.

And completely missed.

Before I could stand, he spun around and stamped on my outstretched leg. The pain was excruciating. He grabbed my ankle and dragged me towards him. With his other arm, he sank his claws into my shoulder then lifted me up over his head. I was totally helpless, flailing like a fish on a hook. He arched his back then hurled me to the floor, forcing the wind from my lungs.

I was face down and he was kneeling on my back, pushing my muzzle into the ground. The pressure was intense. At any moment either my face or my neck would give under the onslaught.

From the corner of my eye, I glanced a flash of gold.

Suddenly there was a huge impact and Dylan was thrown from my back.

I rolled over, to catch sight of my saviour

I knew his scent.

It was Daisy. But how? Daisy wasn't Homo Lupus.

Pearse's stem cell treatment. What did he call it? Lupogenesis.

But there was another surprise to come. I could hear him inside my head.

"This time it's my turn to help you."

He had transitioned. He was full Vukodlak.

I had denied Pearse the activating vector. He must have obtained it from Dylan.

I struggled to my feet. The two giants were locked in combat. Rocking to and fro, they fell to the floor. Rolling over and over in a snarling biting whirlwind of claws and teeth, they left a trail of blood across the concrete.

Abruptly, they broke apart and the golden Wolf hoisted his adversary into the air. He dropped to one knee, and I knew what was about to happen.

It grieved me to see the gentle giant transformed into a killer. "Daisy, no."

"I have to. This can't be allowed to spread. "

He slammed the body of the red Wolf down across his knee and there was a sickening crack. His opponent twitched violently, and was still.

He picked up the corpse by the neck, and dragged it across to where I stood.

"Never again." came the sad voice in my head.

With a shake of his bloodstained muzzle, he dropped the lifeless red Wolf at my feet, turned, and ran off into the night.

Tearing my eyes away from the body, I scanned the immediate area, looking for Annie.

There were fewer Wolves now, and the Vanguard Agents were tightening their cordon.

While the Wolves had the advantage of size, speed and built-in weaponry, like me they had no real combat experience. The Agents stayed out of reach and picked them off from a distance.

Annie was nowhere in sight, so I returned to the spot where the red Wolf had dropped her and searched for her scent.

I followed her trail until I found her, tending to an injured Agent, by the perimeter fence. The top of her skirt was stained with blood, which appeared to have come from under her bullet-proof vest. I pointed to it. She shook her head.

"It's fine, Jack. Really. I'm OK." she put her hand on my shoulder, running it down the fur of my arm. I relaxed a little.

She must have felt guilty about distracting me, as she continued with "Simons says they haven't found Pearse yet. He was last seen by the door, where they all came out. Go. See if you can track him down. Then come back to me."

She took her hand from my arm, and caressed the top of my head. "Good Boy." she added, playfully.

26

Chapter 26

I dropped on to four legs and raced towards the car park entrance. There was no one in sight, but Pearse's scent trail hung in the air, as easy for me to follow as the contrail of a jet plane.

Standing erect, I had to duck to pass under the roller door.

Pearse was not far in front.

I followed the trail downwards. The lights had been turned off.

On the first sublevel, I found Pearse. He was wearing night-vision goggles. He turned to face me.

"Jack? I was hoping it would be you. I wanted to thank you, personally.

If you had not engendered poor Dylan, I could not have completed my work. We could have used his help again, my colleagues and I.

Such a shame that ungrateful tramp brought him to an untimely end. My own fault, I suppose, for endowing him with such a gift. But we had to trial the therapy on someone.

He was our first success."

As he spoke, he was walking sideways, keeping parked cars between us. He needn't have worried. I was quite happy to let him air his rambling delusions before I finally took him in.

There was something else though. The familiar scratching at the back of my brain. Was it Daisy? I'd seen him run off into the night. Not Dylan. He was certainly dead.

Pearse continued "Not wishing to sound, cliched, Jack, but it doesn't have to end like this. My associates will pay handsomely for the promise my breakthrough holds.

And think of the benefits to society. I can now cure all those poor souls who put their trust in my program. Would you deny them the hope of life?"

I had to admit, there was merit in the last point. With the prospect of a bi-centennial lifespan, who was I to deny those less fortunate a chance at longevity?

But it couldn't be on Pearse's terms. For all his preaching, he was only interested in extending one life. His own.

I moved closer.

"Very well, Jack. As you wish."

Even with my enhanced Wolf vision, I didn't see the gun in the dark. There was a dull crack, and I felt a stinging sensation in my left thigh.

Surely he didn't think he could stop me with bullets?

I took another step towards him. Something was wrong. I felt as if my strength were being sapped.

With a grunt, I looked down. There was a hypodart protruding from my leg. A Volsine blocker. I looked back towards Pearse.

"Very kind of Vanguard to provide such a useful little toy. Quite an ingenious gadget. I hadn't counted on them being able to reverse the shift. Lamentably, I shall have to abandon my patients, but my research is complete."

I began to run. Even as a human, I should still be able to overcome a seventy-year-old man. I could follow his scent trail and still find him, even if I couldn't see in the darkness.

"I know what you're thinking, Jack." his voice emanated from the yellow form, glowing in the scentscape "Overpower the Old Man, and save the day. Did you really think it would be so simple?"

The human shape raised a hand to its neck, and my still-sensitive hearing picked up the hiss of a transdermal hypospray.

I knew I was lost. After his success with Daisy, Pearse had taken the stem-cell treatment himself.

He had become Vukodlak.

In the scentscape, the yellow man shape had doubled in size and assumed the form of a Wolf. Pearse's voice was in my head.

"I offered you a chance to join me, Jack. You spurned my hospitality."

The Wolf-shape was coming closer, swinging its muzzle from side to side, following my scent.

"Now nature will take its course. Survival of the fittest, Jack. I will be the new Alpha.

My associates will pay handsomely to share my gift.

We will rule the world, from behind the scenes. "

He continued his rambling mental soliloquy, attempting to divert my attention from the fact that he was edging ever closer.

And then he struck.

As the huge yellow bulk launched itself across the scentscape and leapt on top of the nearest parked car, my body lost the battle with the Volsine blocker. My claws had retracted and my thick pelt was receding. I was beginning to feel the cold.

I also felt afraid and totally alone.

My only chance was to evade Pearse's clutches until help arrived. I dropped to the floor and rolled under the car in front of me. Dragging myself on my elbows and belly, I inched my way to the back of the vehicle. My earpiece had fallen out when I shifted, so I couldn't even call for help.

"Hiding, Jack?" taunted the voice in my head "how very cowardly.

You're only postponing the inevitable."

I rolled again, crossing the gap between the saloon car and its neighbour and taking refuge under a more substantial pickup truck.

There was a grinding, and a crashing of metal, as Pearse rolled the saloon on to its roof.

"You know I can see you, Jack? This scent-sight is really quite remarkable. I pursued the goal of becoming Homo Lupus purely as a matter of survival but I'm beginning to see that it could actually be quite fun.

I don't envisage using the synthetic Volsine again, after tonight. I wouldn't wish to end up a hopeless addict like my unfortunate volunteers but I do think I will be looking forward to the next full moon."

In the darkness, I could 'see' my own scent trail, leading back towards the exit, and safety. It looked a million miles away.

My route across the floor was blocked. The chassis of the next vehicle was too low for even my human frame to slide under.

Pearse was coming closer, sniffing in the darkness. I had to delay him.

"I have to admit, Ambrose, when you told me your plan, I thought you were delusional.

Perhaps Visionary might have been a better assessment. You saw beyond the short-sighted scheming of the Yugoslavs, to use Homo Lupus as a weapon.

They could never have achieved what you've done.

You have the power to resurrect a dying race, to bring it into the light and use it for the benefit of humanity.

Do you really want to begin your journey towards that bright future by killing the only other person in the world who understands what it is to be like you?"

"Apart from our tramp friend, you mean?" I could feel the irony in his projected thoughts.

"I'm sorry Jack, really. I couldn't have done this without you, but I'm afraid Homo Lupus needs a new start, and that must be me.

I will be the father of the new race, and my children will change the world.

And now, much as I have enjoyed our chat, it is time for you to take your leave."

With a groan, the back of the pickup began to rise, the wheels leaving the floor. Pearse held it aloft with one hand, and reached beneath to grab me with the other.

I was naked, apart from my sweat pants, and his claws cut cruelly into the flesh of my leg as he dragged me out and hoisted me into the air.

He dangled me in front of his slavering jaws.

"Goodbye, Mr Allman." The words echoed inside my head, and I closed my eyes.

The sound of multiple gunshots in the underground car park hit my Vukodlak-sensitive ears like a thunderclap.

Pearse shuddered, but maintained his grip. He gave a deep chuckle and turned to face his attacker.

I recognised the scent in the darkness. It was Xander.

He didn't stand a chance. Bullets were not going to stop an eight-foot Werewolf.

"Xander. No. Run!"

He ignored me and fired again. Once, twice. Each shot echoed like thunder around the underground structure.

Dragging me behind him, by my ankle, Pearse leapt towards Xander, covering half the distance in three strides. The rough surface of the concrete floor scraped my exposed skin.

Then he stopped. He coughed. He wheezed.

Releasing his grip, he dropped me to the floor, both clawed hands going to his throat. His breath coming in rasping gasps, he dropped to his knees, shaking his muzzle from side to side. He began to emit a piteous whine, falling forward on all fours.

I could smell his fear. Saliva was dripping from his jaws, and his breathing became more laboured, as he fought to inhale through his rapidly closing airway.

He began pounding at the floor in panic, breaking chunks of concrete with his bloodied fists. Finally, he stood erect and tipped back his head, as if to howl. A barely audible hiss escaped between his clenched fangs and he fell backwards, full length, on the cold stone.

He lay there, unmoving. I could hear his heart beating. Faster and faster, becoming more and more irregular, until it stopped altogether.

Xander kicked the lifeless corpse.

"I told you, Buddy. A bullet is still a bullet." He grinned. "But silver's better."

He took off his overcoat and handed it to me. Wrapping it around, me, I allowed him to help me up the ramp of the car park, and back into the light.

Annie was waiting for me, at the top.

"Aren't you a little chilly, without your fur coat?" she smiled.

"If you have any suggestions as to how to warm me up, I'm all ears."

"Get down, Boy." she warned.

Around us, Vanguard Agents were rounding up the last of Pearse's patients, now all in human form.

Simons and Diego were organising recovery of injured Agents.

"Good show, Mr Allman. I'm sure this is only the first of many operations you will undertake for Vanguard. We will always have a place for someone with your talents.

I'll arrange transport back to HQ for you. We can handle the cleanup, and you're hardly dressed for it.

All of Pearse's research will be confiscated and classified. We don't want it falling into the wrong hands.

I gather one of the Wolves escaped. Apparently after saving your life?

Is he going to be a problem?"

"I don't believe so. Whether we've seen the last of him, I can't say, but I don't see any benefit in pursuing him."

"Very good. Until later, then."

Epilogue

So now, here I am.

There's a hole in my shoulder. Two if you count the exit wound, and I'm feeling pretty brassed off.

We're clearing up the remains of Pearse's alternative research program. His so-called Sangroid option.

Damn, I hate Sangroids. Sure they have an immeasurable lifespan, more than even Pearse aspired to, but they are vile creatures. Shunning the sunlight. Taking sustenance from human blood.

Most people would call them Vampires, and there's a hive of them right beside the river, in a warehouse, owned by Pearse Consolidated.

I tap my comms and speak to Simons, who's running the operation.

"We're taking fire. Permission to deploy Anubis?"

"Permission granted." The words I wanted to hear.

Annie's hormone blocker offered a potential cure for my 'affliction' but I've found my pack now. I have a new family. I belong again.

I'll keep my promise to Hedoen Volkov and never engender another Vukodlak, but I'll continue to use my gift to make the world a safer place for Homo Sapiens.

I visualise the infrapituitary and Volsine begins to course around my body. Looking down, I see the bullet wound healing spontaneously, as the black hairs sprout from the skin around it. My muscles engorge and my claws emerge, like curved razors, ready to wreak mayhem.

I burst from cover and drop to four legs, bounding across the space between my lookout and the warehouse.

Zigzagging, to avoid bullets, I identify the sniper's position.

He'll be my first target.

I twist my muzzle into a wicked grin.

The Sangroids want blood?

I'm the Wolf to show them plenty.

About the Author

David Green was born in Lincolnshire and grew up reading pulp science fiction and watching Hammer horror films.

He now lives in South Yorkshire with his wife and three dogs.

His literary heroes include Isaac Asimov, J.R.R. Tolkien, Jim Butcher, Charlaine Harris and, of course, Terry Pratchett.

His favourite films include Blade Runner, The Rocky Horror Picture Show and An American Werewolf in London.

You can connect with me on:

 http://www.greenhouse.me.uk

 https://www.facebook.com/jackal.man.963

Printed in Poland
by Amazon Fulfillment
Poland Sp. z o.o., Wrocław

61007803R00129